SLEEPWALKERS

Bernie McGill

whittrick
{ PRESS }

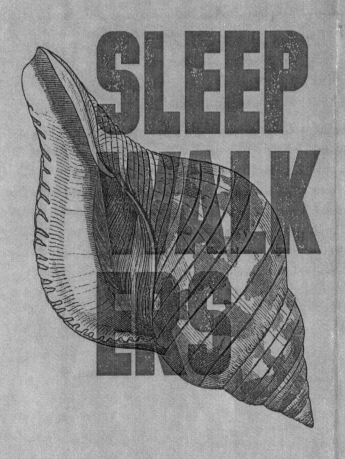

SLEEP WALK ERS

Bernie McGill

Bernie McGill has pursued a diverse career in the arts, as a theatre company manager, writing facilitator and writer for theatre. Her novel *The Butterfly Cabinet*, published by Headline Review in 2010, was widely praised by critics and named by Julian Fellowes, writer of *Downton Abbey*, as his novel of the year in 2012. She was the winner in 2008 of the *Zoetrope: All-Story* Short Fiction Contest in the US and her short stories have been shortlisted for numerous prizes. Bernie lives in Portstewart, Northern Ireland, with her family.

www.berniemcgill.com
twitter.com/berniemcgill

Acknowledgments

'Home' was first published in *The Bridport Prize* (Redcliffe Press, 2010).

'No Angel' first appeared in *Scandal and Other Stories* (Linen Hall Library, 2010); and then in *Southword Journal* in 2011 and in *The Best British Short Stories 2011* (Salt, 2011).

'Sleepwalkers' first appeared in a special online supplement to the Winter 2008/2009 issue of *Zoetrope: All-Story*.

'Islander' and 'The Recipe' were first published in *Verbal*, in 2007 and in 2011, respectively.

A version of 'What I Was Left' first appeared in *Necessary Fiction* in 2011.

'The Bells Were Ringing Out' was first published in *The Ulster Tatler* in 2011.

'Marked' was published in *Good Reading* in 2011.

'First Tooth' was broadcast on BBC Radio Ulster and published in *My Story* (Blackstaff Press, 2006).

First published 2013 by Whittrick Press.
www.whittrickpress.com

A CIP catalogue record for this book is available from the British Library.

ISBN: 978-0-9576080-0-9

Cover Design: www.jeffersandsons.com
This edition published 2013 by Whittrick Press.

Supported by the Creative Industries Innovation Fund.

for John McGill
who knew a thing or two about telling a story

Contents

Home

This is the place. There is a kind of peace, although the cicadas are as loud as tractor engines, and the blood-red dragonflies that hover above the pool worry the air into shuddering rivers of heat. She sits in a recess on the terrace and leans on the low rendered wall, and the ants, interrupted in their single-file trafficking, circumnavigate her freckled elbow as if it were another twig or cone. She has swept up the pine needles, and they lie now in jointed pairs, like unbroken wishbones in piles below the wall. Boats with tucked-up sails line the harbour below; canary yellow kayaks pull up on the limestone rocks.

The house behind is one half terracotta, one half mustard, with wide glazed arches on the ground floor and pale green shutters above. The roof is protected by crescents of pink overlying tiles. Around her, on the circular walls of the raised beds from which pines and olive trees stretch upwards, aching for light, are little mounds of stones and shells and broken tiles, like a child might build for fairy cairns. She had wondered at this at first: the people of the house no longer have young children. Then one day she spots a beetle in beaten metal, blue and green, tunnel its way under one of the mounds. Homes not for fairies, but for insects. What care people will take over tiny crawling creatures, she thinks.

She closes her eyes, tilts back her head, feels the touch of the sun on her eyelids and imagines what it must be like to wake every day, for days on end, without the fear of rain. Nothing real could ever happen in such a place. It does not help that the owners are drapers of fabric: the miniature gazebo to the east of the house is dressed in white muslin so that the sun, when it climbs, shines puddled, blown light on the surface of the green marbled table within. She sits there sometimes in the evenings drinking from a crystal glass, watching the sun dance prisms on her skin. She could be a sea-dweller, living on coral under green water.

To the side of the house is the cottage where she lives now. In the bathroom there is a blue ceramic monkey in a waistcoat and skullcap that lies on its back balancing a soap dish on its four upturned feet. She thinks this is an indignity so she puts her soap on the side of the wash-hand basin where it grows slimy in the wet. When she reaches for it, and her fingernails sink in, she thinks of the thick white candles on the table at Christmas and how Robbie would pinch the molten wax with his small fingers, make indentations that would harden into castellated towers where knights would sleep, he said, and guard the flame until it could be lit again.

The rejection of the soap dish is unusual: in general she likes to keep things tidy. There is no one here to chide or disapprove; the owners have gone and left the place in her care. But it is a way of keeping chaos at bay. She knows, of course, that the stacking of the glasses neck-down on sheets of white rice paper is no guarantee against breakages. She knows that the draught excluder she has pushed against the door will not actually prevent grief from seeping in underneath. But still she does these things because what else is she to do? Drop the glasses onto the floor tiles herself? Swing the door wide to the black night; invite it to come in and hang its coat round her neck, push its feet through her nights? She has done that before and it is no way to live. Now she wipes coasters, places them on tabletops, prevents burn marks on surfaces not equipped to withstand heat. She has taken all the sharp knives out of the cutlery drawer, wrapped them in a tea towel and put them at the back of the cupboard behind the bin. She has surprised herself a little with these efforts to avoid injury. It must mean, mustn't it, that life is worth clinging to? Best not to question that impulse to continue; best not to examine it too closely.

The baker got her this job, caretaking the house for a month while the owners holiday in the States. Easy work, he'd said, sweeping up pine needles, feeding the cat. He'd vouch for her, he said, though she didn't know why, since he hardly knew her – knew her only by one baguette and a croissant each day. She'd watched him in the mornings, a small red-faced man with flour in his grey beard, standing in his white-walled shop at the point where the two long counters met. He knew all the life of the place, dealt out free advice along with *pain au chocolat*, fragrant slices of rosemary-laden pizza. He knew she'd been here too long to be a holidaymaker. This is the danger, she thought, when a man spends his days working transformations. He grows over-acquainted with miracles: pale elastic mixtures that rise into golden loaves; triangular scraps of dough that emerge from the oven, semi-eclipses. It's understandable, she thought, that he should come to believe that heat and time and touch can fix anything. Still, she recognised kindness when she met it. And she had accepted the offer. '*Ça serait bien!*' she had said.

In the cottage now she sweats through the nights, unable to open the windows for fear a mosquito will drone into her sleep, unable to leave the electric fan turning for fear it will overheat and blow all the lights. ('It's a fan,' she hears Sam say in the voice she keeps for him in her head. 'How can a fan overheat?' But still, she sweats through the nights.) One evening, while she is sitting at the table crushing Brie into some bread, the owners' ginger cat brushes past her bare ankle, its touch soft and sudden, before it walks through the hall and onto the terrace. She wants no such invasions, so now she keeps the doors closed all day and the curtains drawn against the heat. She is engaged in a battle with the sun. She favours long skirts, light cotton shirts; within their folds she is growing thin, less of her every day. Each morning she applies sun block to her face, hands and feet, rubs mint-tasting salve into her lips, wraps her head in a blue scarf. She has no desire to be marked. She looks like a person playing at being a nomad, her eyes and skin and hair too pale for someone who has been much exposed to weather. When she is ready, she will move on. No one asks questions in sunny places.

The best time of day is at seven when the lightening room wakes her. She gets up and fills the green kettle with water, the one with the handle that curves up and over the lid like a question mark. She puts it on the hob, before going out to watch the fishing boats return through the neck of the harbour. It is tolerable then, with the moths settling in to the folds of drapery and the cicadas just beginning to thrum. The insects wake, tree by tree with the passage of the sun, falling in and out of rhythm until midday, when their unexpected syncopation vibrates the air above the pines into a burr of static noise. Marseille to the south climbs out of the mist: at seven a grey outline, by noon a

blinding chalk white. The big house watches her, empty. She has
the keys in case of emergencies, but she has no wish to go in.
'Just keep an eye on the place,' they had said, and she does.
Through the glazed arches she eyes the black piano that the
baker has told her plays tunes by itself, the olive tree that grows
up and out through an opening in the roof, that is irrigated each
evening by a punctured hose pipe that snakes its way around
the tree's base. In a recess by the steps that lead down to the sea
door is a blue tiled portrait of St Anthony. She remembers telling
Robbie, when he had misplaced his catapult, that St Anthony
had never failed her. She taught him how to pray and then how
to look, how to go back in his head to where he'd been when he
had last had the thing, to watch himself put it down in the lost
place. He had sat serious for a while, fingers in his dark brown
curls, a frown on his freckled brow, then he'd jumped up and
run to the hay shed where he'd been firing plum stones at the
jackdaws that were picking through grain in the yard. He came
running back, catapult in hand. 'St Anthony's the man!' he'd
shouted to her. She wonders now what lost place he is in.

She is leaning over the stone balustrade into the breeze when
behind her, from the hall of the cottage, she hears a sound that
could be small feet tripping over clay tiles. She walks back in,
hand to her throat, following the sound that grows louder
towards the kitchen. When she reaches it, the kettle has boiled
over, the whistle blown out of the spout, and there are pearls of
water bouncing and skittering all over the glowing hob.

The owners said there was a bicycle in the pool house she
could use. It's a long time since she's been on a bicycle, not since
she was twelve or thirteen when her brothers' bikes would lie
in the farmyard in summer, wheels tilted to the ground, pedals

in the air, like a herd of toppled beasts unable to right themselves. They would spend hours working on them, attaching dynamos and reflectors, submerging inner tubes in basins of water, sharing the thrill when the puncture was found, a fine stream of bubbles breaking the surface. If you were sent for a message, you hoisted one up by the handlebar, swung your leg over, hoped it wasn't the one with the faulty chain that slipped out of its cogs on the upward slope of the hill to Kearnses, when you'd be standing straight up on the pedals, only to come down hard on the bar and then off backwards, your ankles slicked with grease and blood and gravel, the ball bearings bouncing down the hill, reaching home before you. That was the day Sam Kearns found her, brought her and the bike back on the link box of his father's tractor. She smiles at the memory of Sam at sixteen in a navy-blue boiler suit, tall and shy, a crease on his forehead even when he was smiling. And she remembers the look her mother had given them both, at what she must have seen before either she or Sam did. They didn't talk again for years after that. She took off to university, an exchange year in Provence, a teaching job in the city; he took over his father's farm. But it was a gift of a story, the rescue on the link box: it had the stamp of prophesy all over it, was destined from the beginning to be told at a daughter's wedding, and her father didn't disappoint. Nor had Sam kept it from Robbie when he was old enough to hear it.

'Daddy brought you home on his tractor?' he said to her. 'Cool!'

The bike in the pool house at the place in Provence is a lady's bike, black, with a wicker basket in front and a guard on the chain. It makes her feel respectable and at the same time eccentric. She takes it to the supermarket once a week. She could be Mary Poppins, perched on the saddle, flying through the haze of a French afternoon, loaded up with olives and salami (nothing that required heating or stirring), the clink from the basket of a bottle of sauvignon blanc.

This is the way things are the day Harper knocks on the cottage door. He is wiry and American, no taller than she, dressed in a pair of knee-length blue shorts, a white linen shirt, brown leather sandals.

'I'm sorry to disturb you,' he says.

Had she looked disturbed?

'I'm a friend of the family. I stop by from time to time. They don't mind me staying.'

She looks at him. 'They never mentioned that,' she says. Her voice surprises her, the way it's low and rough from lack of use.

'I wasn't planning to be here this trip,' he says. 'They usually leave the key with Monsieur Bapard.'

The name does not register with her. 'Did Sam send you?' but as soon as she says it, she knows how ridiculous this is. Why would Sam send an American?

He looks confused. 'Sam?' he says, 'No, Monsieur Bapard … the baker.'

'Ah!'

'He says there's a cat now. He's allergic? At least I think that's what he said. I won't bother you. I'll sleep in the pool house.'

She knows that he senses her hesitation.

'It's only for a couple of nights,' he says, 'I've done that before.'

He turns and walks towards the pool, his rucksack slung low, his shirt sticking to his back. She locks the cottage door and walks down the hill to the baker.

'*Oui, oui,*' says the baker. '*C'est Harper,*' and the name is suddenly exotic with rolling Rs. '*Il est un ami de la famille. Un artiste. C'est bien.*' He smiles at her, and as another customer enters, dismisses her with a waft of flour.

It is clear that Harper knows the house well. He has found the key to the sea door where it hangs on a hook in the pool house and he walks down the steps, lets himself through. She sees him disappear carrying a towel, knows he'll be down there, diving off the rocks, drifting in the languid sea. She is under the gazebo on his last evening there when he ambles up the steps past St Anthony.

He is leaving tomorrow, stopping at Aix-en-Provence where he is planning to visit the Cézanne exhibition. Would she like to join him for the day? He is younger than her, she thinks, by four or five years.

'I don't think so,' she says.

'I'd appreciate the company, and the help. My French is diabolical.'

'Tomorrow's my day for the supermarket,' she says and as soon as she hears her voice say it, she despises the person she's become.

'Isn't it open every day?' says Harper.

It's years since she's been to Aix. She remembers the baker who knew the house would be good for her, who smiled when he talked about Harper.

'Yes,' she says. 'Maybe I will come.'

In the morning she walks with him to the train station, speaks to the ticket seller, tells Harper they have to change in Marseille.

'This is why I need someone with me,' he says. 'I'd have

stayed on the train until Nice.'

She has brought a book and is relieved to see he has taken one from his rucksack. They sit diagonally opposite each other on the train, but she doesn't read. She looks out the window at the shuttered farm houses and remembers the first time she saw the French countryside and that feeling she'd had then – and still has – when she looks out: that everyone has gone away and closed up their houses, has left them to spiders and beetles, will return at the end of the summer to old webs and the husks of insects.

It's a ten-minute walk from the train station in Aix into town, past moss-grown fountains and market stalls, and the sun is high now. They sit down at a pavement café near the museum. She translates the menu; orders crêpes for him, for her a salade niçoise. Harper sips his water. His hair is dark, curled at his shirt collar, and at his left temple there is a small scar the shape of a hen's foot, livid against his sun-browned face. She would like to put her hand on it, trace the outline with her fingertips, test the depth of it. There is an undertone of winter about his aftershave, something she cannot place – cinnamon, or clove.

He looks up. 'Who's Sam?' he says.

She thinks of all the glib things she could say in answer to that and then looks into her glass and says nothing. She can't find a starting place. She doesn't know how to feel her way back to a beginning. If only I'd left a trail, she thinks, of breadcrumbs, or pebbles.

'I'm sorry,' he says. 'I didn't mean to pry.'

In the crowded, dimly lit rooms of the museum there is no air-conditioning and as they move away from the breeze at the entrance, she feels the walls begin to close in. She struggles to

concentrate on the pictures – white tablecloths, rotting apples, a
skull staring out blank-eyed at her – but it is as if she is viewing
the work through old glass. The images are distorted, grotesque.
She tells Harper not to wait for her, she needs some water; then
she tunnels her way out to the open courtyard and sits down in
the shade of a pine tree. Dark-tinted windows surround her. She
unwraps her hair from the blue scarf and shakes it out, puts a
hand to the back of her damp neck, remembers how to breathe.
She can't see in and she doesn't know if he can see out but
everything she does, she does as if she is being watched. A
woman in a museum uniform is watering the trees, hosing
down the paving, which dries within minutes. A little boy asks
for a turn and the woman hands him the hose to play fireman.
He directs a jet of water at the tree trunk where she is sitting and
a cool spray falls on her hair.

'*Pardon, Madame!*' says the boy's mother and takes back the
hose.

'*Il n'y a pas de quoi,*' she says and smiles at the blond-haired
boy and looks down at her book.

The shadow of the tree moves around the courtyard. She
begins to grow anxious. The last connection leaves Marseille at
eight. She needs to catch the six forty-five to make it on time and
Harper is still somewhere in the museum. She could leave
without speaking to him but instead she waits. At six thirty-five
he comes out.

'I have to run,' she says. 'I'm going to miss the train.'

She's right. She does miss it.

'I'm really sorry,' he says. 'I lost track of time.'

There's a later train to Marseille but no way back to Rouet
from there. They ask about the price of a taxi.

'If you need to go back, I'll pay the fare,' Harper says, 'but it'd be cheaper to stay the night.'

She is tired of always having to save herself. The cat will survive until morning, she decides. One night won't matter. They find a hostel near the station, a bright clean room with four single beds in a row.

'*Il n'y a personne ici*,' says the woman who shows them in.

There's a restaurant down the street. They sit in the garden, share a pizza and a bottle of wine. She looks up from her glass and finds his gaze on her face.

'Why are you here?' he asks.

She considers the question and then she says, 'I don't know where else to be.'

Back at the hostel, she goes into the bathroom and peels off her clothes and stands under the stream of water in the shower. Then she rinses out her underwear in the sink, pulls her skirt and top back on, combs her damp hair through with her fingers. Under the radiator is a pale spider with legs like fine hairs, spinning a fly into a silk cocoon. When she gets back into the room, Harper is lying flat on his back on the bed with the curtains blowing in the breeze. She sits down on the edge of the bed beside him and he reaches up and puts his hand in her hair. She twists towards him, swings her left leg over his body, leans her weight on her hands, lowers herself down. She can feel the hairs on his legs against the damp skin of her thighs. He reaches up and under her shirt, traces the beads of water along her spine, and she leans down, closes his mouth under hers.

She gets up in the night and goes to the window to shut it against the thump of taxi doors and the bars rattling bottles into bins. Harper stirs in the bed behind her. He reaches for her hand.

'Who are you running from?' he says and the answer makes no sense, but she tells him what she knows.

The morning she can't get back to, the one she wants to forget, the one that sits on her mind like a hen on an addled egg, that was the morning Sam took Robbie out to check the animals on the farm. She had said what she always said: 'Go easy on the tractor. No flying over the bumps.' They'd both smiled and saluted her and said, 'Yes, sirree!' and halfway down the green-middled loanen she'd heard Robbie's shrieks of laughter as the vehicle bumped and his head bounced off the tractor seat. They'd gone into the field, Sam told her, with a low mist clinging to the hedges and he could see, a little way down, the humps of three or four of the cattle still sleeping, and he'd thought it strange at the time that they hadn't risen at the sound of the engine. Robbie was in high spirits and had shouted, 'Come on sleepy heads. Come on Blueface, Growler, Slim!' but still the animals hadn't budged, and Sam had a feeling that there was something missing, as they walked down the field together, calling the animals, a line that joined two points, but he couldn't place it, couldn't work out what it was. He was thinking that the sky looked bigger, he said, though he knew that made no sense, and Robbie ran on, calling the animals and then Sam shouted to him to stop. Robbie turned and said, 'What, Daddy?' And there was a noise, a sizzle, like the fat when it hits the hot pan, and a blue spark, and then there was the thing that was missing: the black line that should have divided the sky – except it was on the ground. And then it was rising up out of the grass like a snake's head, with a current along its whole length, whipping high up into the air and falling down now, despite all Sam's shouting, down to where Robbie was standing. Robbie looked at the power cable rearing above him – like it was a surprise his father had arranged for him; like the cows had been in on it, lying low in the field – he looked at the whole blue electric magic show with sheer, unqualified delight, before it came down on his back.

People said it must have been a bird that had snapped the cable, a big one, flying in over the lough – a swan most likely, as if its breed mattered – and that it must have hit at one of the joints and broken the cable in two. But they never found the bird that had done the damage and the three dead cows never spoke. The power company said they were sorry: their automated system had located a fault on the line, had remotely cut off the current that night. But in the morning, to check if it had been a temporary problem, one of the engineers switched it back on and that was when Robbie was in the field. They shouldn't have done that, not without sending someone out to check that the line was intact. It was a very rare occurrence, they said, a freak accident. They assured the public that they had changed their procedures, that nothing of that nature could occur again, but what did she or Sam care about that? After a while of not caring about anything, she packed a little blue suitcase and decided to not care somewhere else – anywhere else, anywhere at all.

In the morning, she and Harper walk to the train station for croissants and coffee. In the bar she takes his hand. She says, 'I can't do this,' and he holds her and then pushes a small paper bag into her hand. He says it's a gift and he touches her hair, and then he smiles and turns and goes. She slips it into her skirt pocket and climbs on to the train.

At the cottage, she puts the green kettle on the hob and goes out onto the terrace where the pot-bound cactus plants lean their spiny tongues toward the sea. The house cat pads past her feet, then stops at the sight of a pigeon strutting by the garden wall. She watches as the cat crouches low, its right ear twitching, mapping the bird as it picks about, gauging the distance, its speed, the bird's wits, devising crucial formulae in its head. Then a boat engine stutters below them and the pigeon flies up, away. She leans out over the stone balustrade. Below her, off the white rocks, a yellow boat is anchored and a grey-haired couple are swimming, their backs to the sun, naked in the sea. She remembers the paper bag in her pocket, takes it out, and inside is a postcard from the museum: a picture of a woman with her hair unbound looking out at the painter like he knows nothing, like she has seen farther than he. In the sea below, the swimmers clamber back into the boat and the woman towels the man's shoulders; he slips a pale blouse over her head and lifts up her damp hair and kisses her face. And she thinks that maybe the baker does know something, after all, about heat and touch and time. And now she can hear the kettle starting to whistle in the kitchen and it won't be long before it spills over again and the beads of water go bouncing over the black hob, looking for all the world like ball bearings off a bicycle chain on a tar road on a warm day, miles and years away from here. And she thinks that if she could follow them, maybe she would find her way home.

The Importance of Being Rhonda

Rhonda's sister is here again, teaching me how to be Rhonda. She brings me a scratch card every visit. She says that Rhonda is a wild woman for the scratch cards, that she'll often buy two or three in one go. She says if Rhonda wins a few quid, she'll go straight back to the shop and buy more cards, and keep going till her luck is exhausted. Rhonda is convinced that one of these days she's going to scratch her way to a fortune. I take the coin she gives me, and though my hand is weak and my grip loose, I scratch and scratch and scratch. The silver film rolls and flakes and drops on the blanket like ash. The symbols emerge, a little blurred – bank notes, spiders, treasure chests, black cats – but she says I need three the same and I don't have enough of the one kind to bring me luck today.

'It's good physio,' she says, 'if nothing else. It's a pity you stayed left-handed.'

I look at the sister, at her black-nyloned legs crossed in the hospital chair, at the white-tipped, straight-cut nails and her two-shades-of-blonde hair. She works, she tells me, at the beauty counter in one of the big stores downtown. She is tinted and blushed and glossed and mascaraed, nothing like the fleshy-faced shorn-headed woman who looks out of the mirror back at me. Seven hours on the operating table, the sister tells me, a walking time bomb, she says, blood pressure and cholesterol through the roof, a bleed on the brain that would have finished most people on the spot.

'It's a good thing it didn't happen at home,' she says, 'we might never have found you.' She brushes the scratchings off the bed cover, puts the coin back in her purse.

The auxiliary comes round with the dinner menu.

'She doesn't like fish,' the sister says. She ticks shepherd's pie, and custard for afters.

I think I might like to try the fish cakes but I don't say anything. What do I know? It's a hard thing to have your meal choices dictated by a woman whose eyebrows are pencilled on.

She has brought me a portable stereo and all of Rhonda's favourite CDs, and she plays them to me and watches my face. There is a smiling man on the cover in a cable-knit jumper. Every song is a lament of some kind, to a lost lover or a dead parent or to God. I try to look willing.

'What does Rhonda want?' I say.

'Want?' says the sister. 'Want? What sort of question is that?'

She looks at me with eyes full of impatience and picks up the chart at the foot of the bed. It's clear that my behaviour is unwarranted. I'm not doing a good job of being Rhonda. On her way out, she stops with the nurses at their station. I watch her tuck her elbows in, extend the palms of her hands to them in a gesture that says, 'How long is this going to take?' They smile, make reassuring noises; she presses the tips of her fingers to her brow. When the click of her heels in the corridor is gone, I tune into Radio 4, listen to a programme called *Money Box Live*.

The doctor comes round, working liquid sanitiser into his hands. This makes me nervous, like something unpleasant is about to happen, some border of decency about to be crossed. Still, he's easy on the eye, tall and dark-haired with a thick black moustache that fails to disguise a harelip. He looks familiar.

'Are you the doctor from *The Clinic*?' I say and he shakes his head. Sometimes, I confuse reality with daytime soaps. I don't think it's a good idea to have a TV in a ward full of brain-injury patients. The flickering images in the white box suspended from the ceiling look like a simulation of what's going on around me.

The doctor leans over to examine the scar on the right side of my head and his fingers are cool. I've seen the graft in the mirror. It looks like a disc of pale wax, like the cooled drippings from a candle, like you could slide your thumbnail underneath and prise it off in one piece without breaking it. I can't help but wonder if Rhonda is trapped underneath. The doctor says it's healing well. He's never known a patient to survive the damage I have. He tells me I'm lucky to be alive. I tell him that's a matter of opinion, and he throws his head back and laughs and I see right up his nostrils, which are cavernous and hairy and dark. That Rhonda fought so hard makes me think that she must have had something to live for, but so far I haven't worked out what that could be. He puts me over it again: what do I remember?

It's not a full picture – it's a kind of shoulder-angle camera shot – but it's all I have for now. I'm on the bus – at least, I think it's me. My left hand is gripping the orange handrail to steady myself as the bus slows, a handbag swings in the crook of my arm. My toe has come out through my sock. There's a whoosh and the doors concertina open and I step down onto the pavement. I see a black suede ankle boot that must be mine, the hem of a navy-blue trouser leg, feel the plastic bag in my right hand knock against my thigh with the weight of what I know to be a packet of ready-made champ. I'm looking forward to it. ('Too much butter and salt,' says the doctor. 'You'll have to cut down on that.') My bra straps cut into my side. My coat won't meet on me. There's snow in the air; the cold grabs at my throat. I see a crushed drinks can trapped in a grating on the road below the kerb with the water pooled on it, the print blurred. And then I feel the cold rush up my left leg under my trousers, like a river travelling up into my arm and into my ear, and then I'm falling and no one catches me and that's what I remember.

What I remember and what I know are not the same and they're both different from what's on TV. I know about the hard skin under the balls of my feet when I shuffle across the floor to the toilet on a walking frame, a nurse's hand at my elbow. I know about the smell of food reheating in the kitchens and underneath that, the smell of ablutions. I can't sleep on my left side: my forearm is tender where they removed the skin for the graft. I wake at the sound the mattress makes when it self-inflates to prevent pressure sores and I feel like the bed is rising into the air like a magic carpet. My nails are short and bare, unshaped. My arms are pale and freckled, bruised at the wrist from where the IVs have been. A delta of blue veins rises on the back of my hand. The skin on my stomach is a little loose, like it has been stretched over a larger woman.

I open my eyes and there's the sister again, sitting on the blanket on the bed. She knows she's not supposed to do that – it carries infection in – but there's someone else in the hospital chair. She introduces a pale girl wearing a black corset over a dark green dress. She says this is the niece. The niece's lips are painted black. Her hair is black, too, and hangs down over her shoulders, but with a green streak pinned back with a single hairgrip behind her right ear. There is a black crucifix at her throat. Her eyelids are shaded red. She looks up from her phone and smiles, and the two black studs pierced into her lower lip move a little further apart. Her thumbs are busy the whole time at the phone. She could be the angel of death. The sister puts her hand over mine.

'She's your god-daughter,' she says.

The niece goes on tapping.

The sister is here to tell me stories. Rhonda has a little terrace house that backs on to the railway lines not far from here. Rhonda used to work in the cigarette factory; she got a job as a cleaner when the factory closed down. Rhonda's much sought-after, the sister says; she has keys to houses off the Malone Road; she's known to be very particular. Rhonda keeps old toothbrushes and dips them in bleach and cleans the grouting between the shower tiles in the bathrooms of the people who can afford her. The sister says she does for her too, though Rhonda won't take a penny for it, of course; Rhonda's the kind of person who would give you the shirt off her back. Rhonda saved every penny she had and took the sister and the niece to Venice last summer; she wouldn't hear of them paying for a thing. She produces a photograph: Rhonda seated in a gondola with round cheeks and plump arms in a vest-top that wrinkles over her belly, white cut-off trousers that show blue-veined legs. I look at the niece, trying to picture her in sunlight and fail. The sister takes a small silver-wrapped parcel out of her bag, presses it into my hand.

'Here,' she says, 'you missed Christmas.'

I struggle to open it. It is a piece of clouded glass, no bigger than my thumb, in the shape of a zebra, gold stripes down its side. The sister says Rhonda collects glass ornaments; she has a cabinet full of them in her house. She had them affronted at the stalls in St Mark's Square, haggling with the vendors over pieces of glass.

'Isn't that right?' says the sister to the niece.

The niece lifts her head, says they never have any trouble knowing what to get for Rhonda.

The sister says I'm failed, I need to build myself up, try and eat the food, such as it is. I say there's nothing wrong with the food, it's a pleasure to have something set down in front of you, and she twitches her lipstick lips at me and says it'll be good to have Rhonda back. The niece's phone buzzes and she's at it again, black-painted nails sending coded messages, smiling at the replies. I wonder what they both look like untouched.

'Does Rhonda live a fulsome life?' I ask.

'Fulsome?' says the sister, and the niece laughs down her nose at the phone. 'Fulsome? Where'd you get a word like that?'

I twist in the bed. 'My feet are cold,' I say, and this produces an actual smile.

'Sure your feet are never warm,' the sister says. Before she goes she whispers to me that the niece is getting on great in school. 'She's doing her A Levels this year,' she says. 'She'll be looking at universities soon.' She stands up and sighs, straightens the bed cover. 'And you know that doesn't come cheap,' she says.

I don't know this but I don't say anything. I wait until they're gone. Then I wrap the zebra in a tissue and slip it down the side of the bed-frame and listen for the moment when the mattress re-inflates and I hear the glass animal splinter.

There's a screen print in the corridor on the way to x-ray of a black cat seated by a red wall. You can tell it's been deliberately misprinted: the blocks of colour don't tally with the outlines; it looks like you're seeing double. It makes me think of those badly printed cartoon strips you used to see in the papers. But if you asked anyone to say what it was, they'd say, 'That's a black cat.' It's recognisable by its pointed ears, slanted white eyes, curled tail. We're a poor fit, me and Rhonda, our contours don't quite match. I haven't found anything in her yet to like. I can't help but wonder if she's going about her business somewhere parallel to me. And now I know a new thing. I'm not climbing back inside the shell of that woman they want me to be.

I turn down the blanket and find the label and stroke the silk with my fingers. The washing instructions are out of focus in a language I don't understand. I take comfort from the symbols: a tub with a squiggly surface of water, a triangle crossed by an X, a dot in a circle in a square. The clarity and the ease of it: the things you can and cannot do; directions about how to behave. They remind me of the symbols on the bottles of bleach I've seen the hospital cleaners use: a thick black X, a skull and crossbones, a black and orange flame.

The porter arrives on the ward with a trolley clinking with jugs of fresh water, and the physio assistant comes in, the girl with the dark brown eyes. She says I'm getting stronger every day; we're going to try some writing. She's brought me a pen enclosed in soft foam to improve my grip and a clipboard with grey ruled notepad pages.

'Do you wear glasses?' she asks.

'How would I know?' I say, and she laughs and says that with my permission she'll look in the locker, see what's there.

She brings out a black leather-look handbag, the plastic

showing through a worn gold-coloured clasp. Inside is a scabbard and a pair of glasses, and when I put them on, the washing instructions and the symbols on the label sharpen into focus. There's a purse in the bag with a few loose coins, a bus pass, a bunch of keys. And there's a small pocket-sized savings book in Rhonda's name, with an amount in the balance column that must be ten times what she earns cleaning in a year.

Jingle-jangle go the jugs as the porter trundles from bed to bed replacing the water on the hospital trays. And as he passes me, a room swims into view, a corner cabinet, shelves arranged with glass objects that shiver and tremble each time the train goes past on the railway bridge above. There's a scratch card on a blue formica-topped table, something like silvered ash scattered round, three black cats with pointed ears, their tails curled, lining up for a perfect match.

'Can you just try writing your name?' the physio says. 'I know it will be hard at first.'

It is hard but I concentrate. I balance the clipboard on my legs, steady it with my right hand. I pick up the pen, squeeze the foam between my thumb and forefinger, angle it at the lines on the pad. I make a mark; the pen bleeds a little, black ink clots on the page. It's like a child's hand, a first attempt at joined-up writing, the letters backwards-leaning, ugly, ill-formed. But with a bit of effort and a little time I find that I am able to form the outline of 'Rhonda'.

The Language Thing

You are standing cold on the platform in Ancona waiting for Kerry to come. It is late March, past nine in the evening, and the station is almost deserted. If the train is delayed, or she is not on the train, you will have no way of knowing where she is, because this is 1988 and you have never seen a mobile phone. You are Language Assistants on your year out, Kerry in Germany, you in Italy. She has written to say she will arrive today. You have bought butchers' sausages and *passata* to make the only dish you know. The butcher near the school sells *caciocavallo*, that smoked cheese you like, but on days when you are lazy with your consonants and stress the wrong syllable, you say something that translates as cabbage-penis, and although the butcher smiles and is polite, you just can't take the risk. It's a minefield, the language thing.

There is no fridge in your rented second-floor flat but you have left a bottle of *Verdicchio* cooling in the big white water-filled sink, and for dessert there is a parcel from the *pasticceria*, tied with brown ribbon, containing *bigne, bomboloni*. You like to watch the girl in the shop as she curls the ribbon with the blade of the scissors, lets it drop in ringlets down either side. You like the Italian attention to detail, the way this is not considered a trivial thing. The windows in your flat have metal shutters; the walls could do with a lick of paint. You have pasted your collection of postcards round the frames: images of window pots and painted half-doors. You have always had a liking for scenes glimpsed through openings, the hinted-at lives lived beyond. Your walls are papered with photocopied cut-outs of James Dean. There is a wipe-clean tablecloth with an ivy design. There is no phone in the flat, and once a week you walk to the SIP and queue with the other foreigners to make an expensive call home from one of the cubicles there. Sometimes you see Milton, the Nigerian student. He says you have a lot in common because he saw you once in the library with a copy of *Paradise Lost*. He tried to follow you home but you lost him on the *corso*. You are all strangers here but you prefer to be alone.

The Italian that's spoken on the radio and on your crackly black-and-white television that shows only *Rai Uno* is too rapid for you to understand, although you catch a word here and there. The teachers at the school say you must come to dinner, but they don't give you their addresses and they don't say when. You listen to cassettes of Everything But The Girl and you write long letters to friends posted around Europe. The delay in replies is often three weeks long. The internet is unknown to you. In no way could you be said to be current. When Signor Mori, the history teacher at the *Liceo*, says something in Italian about *Irlanda del Nord* you nod and agree that things there are bad. Once, he tried to engage you on the subject of Cromwell but you made your excuses and slipped off to your class. You are uneasy in the role of ambassador. Neither your knowledge of history nor your command of the language is of a standard for political debate.

There is a group of boys hanging out round the station and

still no sign of the train. You don't recognise them, though they are the age of some of the oldest students in your school, and perhaps only a year or two younger than yourself. One of them casts a glance your way. You don't understand how they can tell that you are foreign. Some Italians have skin and hair as pale as yours, but they know just to look at you that you're not from here. Something to do with the cut of your cloth. A whistle sounds, lights approach up the dark line and then there's Kerry, standing on the platform with a newspaper in her hand, fragile.

'Have you seen this?' she says, and she hands you the paper.

She had to change trains in Venice, where the headline caught her eye. She doesn't have much Italian, but the pictures need no translating. You see a body on the ground, a priest on his knees, catch the word 'Belfast', before the boys close in.

Kerry's appearance is all the encouragement they need. They walk up and in their accents say, 'Hello. How are you?' assuming you're English, stressing their aitches the way they've been taught. Kerry gives you an unmistakable look. You can tell she's not in the mood.

'Have you learnt how to say, "Piss off"?' she mutters.

'There's no point,' you tell her, 'it'll only egg them on.'

'Where are you from?' says one boy, light-haired, dark-skinned, targeting Kerry. 'London?' he says, 'Liverpool?'

Kerry turns to you, her expression a little changed. 'As Gaeilge?' she says.

You are winded by this. It's years since you've spoken Irish, and you didn't do it well at the time. You reach back seven years to Mr Keenan's class, to closing doors and opening windows and placing teapots on stoves, to the declension tests for which you and Kerry had devised an elaborate cheat. None of this is of any use to you now, standing at the station in Ancona, being asked to use the language as a shield. Then something comes, the one thing no Irish scholar ever forgets.

'*Ár n-Athair*?' you say to Kerry, '*atá ar neamh*?'

She winces, but only slightly. 'Hallowed be thy name,' she answers in Irish.

The boys look confused. '*Svedese*?' asks the light-haired one. 'Swedish?'

'*Go dtaga do ríocht*,' you say to Kerry, leading the way towards the bus stop outside the station.

'Thy will be done,' she replies in Irish, 'on earth as it is in heaven.'

The boy, following, turns to his friend: '*Olandese*? Dutch?'

Kerry smiles, beginning to enjoy herself a little, directs a question at the boy himself, as if trying to help: '*Ár n-arán laethúil tabhair dúinn inniu*?'

'And forgive us our trespasses,' you say, looking at him too, unsettling him. 'As we forgive those who trespass against us.'

'*Ach ná lig sinn I gcathú*,' says Kerry, shaking her head.

'But deliver us from evil,' you say back in Irish, and then the last bus arrives for Jesi, and delivers you both.

'Sacrilege,' Kerry says on board. 'Using the Our Father for a purpose for which it was never intended. What would Father Tony say?'

'It was either that or *Báidín Fheilimí*,' you say, 'and I can't remember that without singing it.'

'This much we are spared.'

You are glad to have lightened the mood, but you know that it is temporary. She looks down at the newspaper again.

'"Savages!"' she says. 'Isn't that what it means?'

You nod. 'When did it happen?'

'Yesterday, I think. I can't believe the pictures. Do you think those have been in the papers at home?'

You take the paper from her. Newspaper Italian is difficult for you but you understand more than you want. The priest has his hands joined, his brow furrowed; he is looking down on the upturned face of the man on the ground. The man is on his back, spread-eagled, his face turned away from the camera. He is naked to the waist, his ribs visible, his legs and feet are bare. The picture is in black and white but there is no mistaking the marks on the body, on the head. Even from this angle you can tell it would not have been an easy face to look on.

'What does it say?' Kerry asks.

What you make out is that it happened at a funeral, the mourners nervous; the man being buried had been shot in an attack in a graveyard, at another funeral, a few days before. It's very hard at this distance, through this language, to make sense of it. You give her the decoded details.

There is a long silence on the bus between you.

'There are soldiers' kids in my school,' Kerry finally says.

You walk through the dark from the bus stop in Jesi, up the stepped hill past the mediaeval towers and buttressed walls and onto the *corso* that is beginning now to empty of the usual Sunday night walkers. The cafés and bars are closing up, people hurrying home to their families. You climb the cold steps to the flat together, race the timed light to the second floor, insert the key in the door just as the darkness returns.

You cook and eat and talk about what you miss: the leaves on University Square in October, the echo of your heels on the tiles when you walk through the Lanyon at night, the glar on the

floor of the Crescent and all of you singing at the tops of your
voices to The Waterboys. You get out the map and draw a line
to connect you, you and your displaced compatriots – from
Belfast to Bielefeld to Mantova and Jesi, to Valencia and Limoux
and back – and it forms the outline of a misshapen square, a box
bent out of kilter. You are at odds, all of you, with the places in
which you find yourselves. You are at odds when you're at
home. You don't talk any more about the newspaper, or the
picture, or the words, or what you'll say when you go back to
your schools, or what will be said back to you. You pour the
wine into short, coloured tumblers and you toast the accidents
of history and language that brought you here. And you slide a
cassette into the player you bought with your first month's
wages and you listen together in the dim light of a strange
country to the voice of an English girl. She's in Italy, she sings,
with a sunhat and a dictionary, but she's lonesome for a place
she knows.

No Angel

The first time I saw my father after he died I was in the shower, hair plastered with conditioner, when the water stuttered and turned cold. He was at the sink in front of the misted-up mirror with the tap running, his back to me. It was two weeks after his funeral. His things were all where he'd left them.

'Them tiles would need re-grouting,' he said, and pointed his razor at the salmon pink mould that was growing below the mirror.

I stared at him through the circle I'd wiped in the shower door. 'I didn't know you'd be able to do that,' I said.

'Oh yes,' he said, 'any decent tradesman would sort that out for you.' The twitch of a smile; thran as before.

He looked more or less the same. When he turned his face to scrape the razor along his jaw I could see that the scar was healing well where the surgeon had removed the growth from the side of his nose. His skin was still yellow at the nicotine-stained finger tips.

'Are they treating you well?' I asked him.

'So, so. The food's not great. Nothing seems to have much of a taste.'

'I suppose you empty the salt cellar over it still?'

'What harm's it going to do me now?'

I looked at him, at the thin white hair curling at the back of his neck from the steam in the bathroom, the earth under his fingernails.

'I'm getting cold,' I said.

'Don't worry,' he said, bending to splash water on his face, his knees creaking, 'I'm going now anyway,' and away he went.

The next time I saw him I was on the train on the way to Belfast, sitting opposite a girl in a green bobble hat; his face appeared in the window to my left. I looked back at the girl in her small round glasses, breaking off squares of chocolate with her teeth, at the umbilical iPod threading its way from ear to pocket. But outside, reflected in the glass, it was his face skimming over the fields. It was early December; there was a skin of snow on the hedges, green showing through, a slick of ice on the flooded grass. A bad time to spread slurry, he would have said. I'd never been on a train with him before.

'We used to ride to Knockarlet,' he said, smiling his crooked smile, showing a bottom row of neglected teeth. 'Me and your mother. Left the bikes at the station and took the train to the Port for the Big Sunday. It's years since I was on a train.'

He spoke the way he had always spoken in his later years, like he was suppressing wind, like the next sound that emitted from his mouth might be an involuntary one. People used to finish his sentences: he made them nervous of what was going to come out.

I loved that photo we had in the house, the pair of them strolling down the prom arm in arm, her in her swing coat and curled hair, him in his wide lapels, a cigarette hanging off his right hand. They looked like film stars, the ghosts of their young selves. I used to pore over it as a teenager, wondering who they had been then, before me and then Jamesie were born into their lives, before we wrenched love from them, and left again.

Above his head in the train window were mirrored the orange letters of the information screen: 'Attention please. Passengers without a valid ticket please purchase one from the conductor.' He looked up, stuck out his elbow, nudged no one in particular, winked in at me.

'Never let on you saw me!' he said.

Christmas week I was invited out to dinner with Thomas's parents. Situation vacant: prospective daughter-in-law. I watched them process my details – a good lecturing job, attentive, soft-spoken, a bit long in the tooth for grandchildren possibly, but these days you never know. They were far too middle-class for religion to be an issue. The restaurant was over-heated; I'd gulped down too many glasses of *pinot grigio* and had stepped outside for a breath of air. Daddy legged it out from a bus shelter on the far side of the road, dodged over between breaks in the headlights, a greasy brown paper bag in his hand.

'Are you going to marry thawn boy?' he said. Not so much as a 'Hullo'.

'You know his name, Daddy.'

'Are you going to marry him?'

'He hasn't asked me.'

He sighed through his nose, and his breath came out in two puffs of mist. 'I never knew you were that oul-fashioned,' he said. The smell of chip fat and vinegar.

'What's in the bag?' I asked him.

'You didn't answer me.'

'Neither did you.'

A couple came out the restaurant door; a blast of voices and heat, garlic and alcohol.

'He'll never set foot on my farm,' he said.

'He's a Maths teacher, Daddy. He doesn't want your farm.'

'He says that now,' he grunted. 'But they're all the same – hungry land grabbers every last one of them. He'll not get it. Not after what we went through to keep it.' He wrung the paper bag into a twist, fired it into a nearby bin.

'Not everybody's after your land, Daddy.'

'Have you forgotten what they did to your brother, Annie? The way they left him, lying on the road like a bag of rubbish the binmen had forgotten to lift? What it did to your mother, to see him like that?'

I gritted my teeth. 'It wasn't Thomas did that.'

'Him or his kind. I make no difference between them.' The spit flew out of his mouth. Then he turned on his heel and strode down the street, some loose change heavy in the outside pocket of his green fleece, banging against his thigh, altering the hang of him. It had never occurred to me that the dead could be bitter still, could still feel loss.

My brother Jamesie wasn't the son my father had had in mind for himself. Daddy was a teetotaller all his life; the only drink we ever had in the house was a drop of poteen he kept for a sick cow. And my father was quiet, rarely raised his voice, except maybe to curse at a referee, or a traffic warden. Jamesie, on the other hand, was loud, drank too much, lost all his money on poker machines, stole fags out of Daddy's coat pocket, took no interest in cattle rearing. He had a great sense of himself as unquashable, shot his mouth off when the rest of us knew how to stay dumb; he had never learnt caution the way most people had in our uneasy mixed community. Some of the time I admired him for it, wished I could speak without looking to the left and right of me first. He wasn't involved in anything – people round here would have known that – if he had been, Daddy would have knocked it out of him himself. All he wanted was to join a rock band and 'get the hell out of this backwater'. The eighties were a nervous time, and things were worse after something big: Loughgall, Enniskillen, Milltown, Ballygawley. Those were the times when people walked about careful, eyes to the ground. Jamesie never eyed the ground. You'd think, then, he'd have seen it coming, what hit him in the face. A mallet, the coroner said, the type that was used to bash in fenceposts. They never found it.

Strange thing, though, he walked like Daddy: shoulders forward, great loping strides. Three years younger than me and every step of his was one and a half of mine. I could never keep up with him. He was seventeen and built like a stick and mad about his guitar. He'd just failed his driving test and had called in the pub, where he shouldn't have been, and was walking home. They must have followed him out. It was December, dark by four and bone-cold. The coroner said he thought a car had hit him – after the beating, when he had been left on the road. He couldn't be sure but there was evidence the body had been dragged. It was a neighbour that found him, picked him out in the car headlights. Daddy insisted on an open coffin, despite Jamesie's eyebrow like a burst plum, his buckled nose, the rainbow of bruises that spanned his battered face. Despite Mum saying, 'Let people remember him the way he was.'

'No,' he said. 'Let everybody see what they did to him. Let everybody look and know what animals we're living amongst.'

They never got anybody for it, but ever since, there have been neighbours of ours that couldn't look us in the eye. Mum lasted six months of barely speaking, food hardly passing her lips. She dropped like a stone one day in the kitchen: never spoke again.

'Your mother,' Daddy said to me, like he had to apologise for her leaving, '… her heart never mended.'

Then it was just me and him, for nearly twenty-two years, until his lungs gave way and the breath left him too.

In one of the bad times, around Hallowe'en, a month or two before Jamesie was killed, I was home from university and Mum asked me to go in the front room and bring her in the sewing basket that she kept under the bed. I knelt down on the burgundy carpet, lifted the valance sheet, and there was the shotgun, quiet as you like. Daddy had always kept one: he and Uncle Joe went shooting for pheasant every Boxing Day. And if there was a wedding in the townland, he'd take it out, shoot a cartridge or two in the air to send the bride off. But the rest of the time, he kept it locked up in the built-in wardrobe. He was normally very careful about it. I carried the basket back in to the kitchen.

'Why's the gun under your bed?'

'Thread that for me, will you?' she said.

She sat with Daddy's good trousers on her lap, pressing the unravelled hem between her finger and thumb. I held the needle up to the light, laced the grey thread through.

'Two or three times,' she said, 'a car has driven into the yard at night. No lights; we hear the wheels on the gravel.' She took the needle from me, wound a knot into the end of the thread. 'Your father says if any of them tries to get in, he'll shoot first, ask questions later.'

'Why would anybody …?'

'There's people, Annie, that needs no excuse. We're the wrong sort for them, that's all – in the wrong place. They'd like to see the back of us.' And she pushed the needle into the hem and started to sew.

I was glad to get back to Belfast. The threat in the city never felt personal. A bomb scare on University Road and everybody piled back into bed, lectures cancelled for the morning. The night the explosion went off at the Lisburn Road police station, the whole of our rented house shook. Eight girls on the landing in their pyjamas and then down to the kitchen to stand bare-footed on the cracked, snail-slimed lino, warming our hands around cups of tea, listening for the sirens; second-hand drama. Not like a dark car in your own yard at night; not like a shotgun under the bed.

The next time I saw my father after he died it was night and I was driving over the bog road near Castlenagree, with the windscreen wipers doing battle against the rain and Bob Dylan on the radio: 'Like a Rolling Stone'. I'd turned the music up full and was giving it welly: 'How does it feel …?'

'What's that oul' shite you're listening to?' he said, and near put me off the road. A twitter of a laugh. 'That would deave you,' and his hand reached out and turned down the dial. The dashboard gave off a green light; my fists were tight on the steering wheel. 'What happened your hand?' he said. A small black crescent of soot was ingrained above my knuckles.

'You know rightly what happened it,' I told him, 'putting the life out of me in the coal house last night. I hit it against the shovel.' He was silent. The sound of his skin-roughened finger and thumb, rubbing together. 'Knocking the door against the back of my heels,' I said. 'You know I don't like the dark.'

'It was maybe the wind.'

'There wasn't a breath. You needn't deny it. I smelt Benson and Hedges.'

'I've given up the smokes,' he said. 'They were a shocking price, getting.'

'Your timing's not great.'

The rain was coming down harder, troughing water along the sides of the road. I could smell the damp wool of his jacket drying in the fan, and something underneath it, something familiar – coal tar soap.

'Does this seat not go back?' he said, grappling for the lever at the side. 'That Thomas boy must be a right short-arse. My knees is killing me.'

I was silent, not rising to the bait, and then, 'Do you remember,' he said, 'the night you swallowed the two-p bit?'

I did. I was five, six maybe. I can still feel the chink of metal against my teeth, taste the copper, feel the wrong shape of it slide down my throat. I don't know what upset me more: the swallowing of it, or the disappointment at the loss of the money. I hadn't made the connection between food and waste; I was stunned when Mum said I wasn't to flush the toilet till she was sure it had passed. And every morning, the same line from him and Jamesie …

'Any change?' he said in the seat beside me, his whole body shaking.

That was the night he told me the story of Ali Baba and the Forty Thieves. And when he reached the part about the robbers hiding in the urns, I didn't know the word, so he said, 'You know, urns, big containers, like tea chests. That's what we'll call them. The thirty-nine robbers hid in the tea chests and the captain went into the house.' It was nearly worth swallowing the coin for: the candy-striped sheets in their big bed and the light coming in under the crack in the door, and Ali Baba in his turban and the blind cobbler and the clever servant-girl, and the robbers in the tea chests. And the burst-open brother they had to sew back together again.

'You know, Annie, I would never scare you like that. That wasn't me at the coal house door.'

I kept my eyes on the road as we rounded a bend. Then I said, 'Daddy, do you ever see …?' but when I turned my head, the seat beside me was empty.

He needn't have bothered with the jibes about Thomas: we didn't last. I think it was Thomas's confidence I fell for – his belief in my ability to love him back, his faith in the world's acceptance of us both. He never questioned his right to be anywhere. He was entirely without arrogance but he stood and talked and put one foot after the other with absolute unshakeable conviction. I think, maybe, if I'm honest, he reminded me of Jamesie. It was never going to work. I couldn't have kept up the suitable daughter-in-law show for a whole lifetime.

Daddy made occasional appearances after that. One Tuesday afternoon after the spring term had started, I looked out from a lecture hall of second-year students who cared little for Molière or the Commedia dell'Arte and I saw him, intent, climbing a grass bank, heading towards the University Arboretum with a hazel stick in his hand, his corduroy trousers bagging at the knees. I got the impression he was following someone.

Then one night in May at the Opera House – a staff outing to *The Bartered Bride* and me bored witless – I tore my eyes away from Marenka in her embroidered apron and glanced up at the boxes, and there he was: good grey suit, opera glasses in his hand. He who had never set foot in a theatre in his life.

'What are you doing here?' I mouthed up at him.

'Keeping an eye on him,' he said, and he stuck out his elbow and nudged the man beside him: Jamesie, in an oversized bow tie, with his face back the way it used to be. 'I told you it wasn't me at the coal house door.'

Jamesie was scanning the audience. 'There she is,' he said, and pointed to a small woman three rows ahead in a turquoise dress with winged shoulder pads. The woman turned and looked up and waved: Mum out in her finery. Neither she nor Jamesie looked at me.

'You found them,' I said.

'I did,' Daddy said.

'They look well.'

He nodded and smiled.

'Will you leave me alone now?' I asked him.

He looked down at his hands. 'I was right about thawn Thomas boy,' he said. 'He wasn't your match.'

'I won't be told who to love by you,' I said.

'I know.'

I looked around at the packed auditorium, at Mum's shining eyes, back up at him and Jamesie. 'I'll see you, then,' I said.

I could see his mouth move: 'You know where we are.' And then the song ended, and the audience rose up in applause and blocked my view with their bellowing elbows and the backs of their nodding heads.

Sleepwalkers

There are four of them. Kate, the mother, a little dazed by the ferocity of the Andalusian sun, and her three brave children: Marcus, Abigail, Florrie. They are bundled with their luggage into a silver Ford Fusion and they are driving slowly along the coast road through Torremolinos and Benalmádena, past the clutter of signs for aquaparks and English breakfasts. The children's eyes are wide at the blue-tinted images of giant hydro slides, but they are good children and they have an idea of how much energy she has and they don't ask. Florrie is eight, still capable of finding wonder everywhere she looks. 'Wow!' she says at a thick-trunked palm. 'Look at the size of that pineapple!'

Kate has memorised the directions, but Marcus, fourteen and important, unfamiliar on her right-hand side, has the map on his knee, and so as to hear his voice now, she asks him where they are. She is not too distressed at their having lost the motorway; they are travelling in the right direction, after all, just a little more slowly. She wasn't quite ready for the impact of the *autopista*: hundreds of tourists in hired cars speeding along on the wrong side of strange roads.

The road up to Ronda, when they find it, is terrifying. Cut into the mountainside, it winds its way up for almost an hour. At a narrow plateau, a dark-dressed woman is selling watermelons and Kate pulls in. She buys one, gestures for the woman to cut it, and they stand on the roadside eating slices, the red juice sliding down their necks, spitting the dark seeds into the dust. She spots Abigail wipe a seed clean, slip it into her pocket, a fossilised raindrop. Abigail is twelve and intense; records must be kept of every experience.

Raquel's directions are good: they find the turn off the main road from Ronda to Seville, drive under the railway arch, and along the laneway to the sign at the gate: *Finca Los Nogales*. Inside, there are cobwebs in the cupboards and dead flies in all the corners. Kate lifts a glass from the press in the kitchen and it sticks, momentarily, to the tacky shelf. The plates on the dresser are aqua blue, with engravings of leaves and fish, and are covered in a thin, greasy film of dust. The drawers rattle with candles and loose nails, and are scattered with dead beetles, crumbs. The unglazed tiles are stained with tomato juice and with something darker. The pantry is lined with things that other visitors have left: olive oil and balsamic vinegar; something called '*Brillante: el arroz que no se pasa*'; camomile tea bags; sachets of saffron stock for paella; cartons of UHT milk. There is no hot water. She consults her phrase book and phones the number that Raquel has given her for her cousin José who looks after the place. When a man's voice answers she says the name of the house and then, '*No agua caliente*' and presses the call-end button before he can speak, since nothing he can say will mean anything to her.

They have packed their costumes in their hand baggage and the children have changed, impatient for the pool. They swim, all three of them, like eels, but they have promised to wait for her. She walks behind them up the path from the garden door, and before she even reaches the railings that surround the pool, they are through the gate and in. Florrie is at the side, holding on, kicking her feet out behind her; Marcus has divebombed into the centre; Abigail is treading water, legs cycling, arms in a figure of eight.

'It's lovely, Mammo,' cries Florrie. 'Come in!'

'Everyone to the side while I check the depth,' Kate says, and she slips into the sun-warmed water without a single intake of breath, an act of almost total immersion.

She walks the whole way round and it's the same everywhere: five feet deep. She stands watching the swifts fly back and forth, casting shadows like grenades over the pool and garden, and wonders how she came to be here, up to her neck in water, without any language to speak of. Her girls are doing water ballet, touching their toes, twirling around; then Florrie swims over and she balances the child on her arm.

Florrie says, 'Am I heavy, Mammo?' and Kate replies, 'Not one bit.'

José arrives around six, calling '*Hola*' from the gate, and they haul themselves out and troop, dripping, down to the garden door. He seems a kind man, with too many teeth in his head, which make him look like he is always smiling, which perhaps he is. He takes the cover from the front of an ancient boiler in the wash room and before long there is a whooshing sound and water in the tap that is a few degrees above lukewarm. When his phone rings, and he answers it to a woman's voice, he says, '*Con la viuda*' and she knows the word, because she looked it up before they left, just in case she was asked. She is glad that Raquel has told him this; it has more dignity – and strictly speaking, she is a widow, since Owen managed to kill himself before she managed to divorce him. As José is leaving, he points to a towel Marcus has left on the lawn, says something more about the water and something else about lights and, uncomprehending, she says '*Gracias*,' and then he's gone.

The children have found a portable CD player, covered in grass cuttings from where it's been left out, and Florrie is dancing around the salon on one leg, singing along to something light and drummy. Kate goes into the kitchen, too tired now to face the dusty trek to the supermarket, and concocts a dinner out of what other people have left behind. The children dip rice cakes in *passata* and eat, their eyes heavy with sleep. She tucks them each into the beds that José's wife has made up for them.

'Tomorrow,' she says, 'will be a day of eating what you want.'

She leaves the hall light on, closes her bedroom door to a crack and opens all the windows wide. The two-hundred-year-old walls have soaked up fifteen hours of heat. There are lights on now in the garden and they cast barred shadows on to the wall at the foot of her bed. She falls asleep and dreams that she and Owen are on the plane, flying to Malaga; and it is falling out of the sky, the sound of the engines and of the nearing ground, roaring in her ears. She jumps awake, upright in the bed, her heart thumping, and the sound carries on, growing louder with every beat, coming right into the room. And then it is a freight train, as loud as a crash, taking minutes to pass high up on the bank above the house, over the railway arch, whistling on past the window in the gable. She swings her legs out of bed, finds the water she left on the wicker-top table, her mouth making a cave echo over the top of the glass. On the table there is a little round alarm clock, the size of Florrie's fist, with green fluorescent numerals and hands. The time is five past four. Not trusting the floor, she searches with her feet for her espadrilles and pads out into the hall to check on the children. The girls are sleeping side by side in twin beds, Florrie spread-eagled in a pair of pink knickers, Abigail curled up in a tee shirt.

In Marcus's room, at the head of the stairs, the sheet is crumpled to the foot of the bed but there is no sign of the boy, on either side or underneath, and the bathroom too is empty, the naked bulb shining bright. From outside, she thinks she can hear the tinkle of water. Halfway down the stairs she sees that the door into the garden is open, that there are wet footprints that stop on the path leading up to the pool. When she goes out, Marcus is lying on the short green grass under jets of water that the sprinklers are arcing across the lawn. The towel he left there is soaked. He raises a hand to her.

'*Agua*!' he calls. '*Agua*! It's too hot!'

She sits down on a plastic garden seat, the cold of it a shock on her bare legs, and listens to the grinding of the cicadas. And though it isn't anywhere near light, a rooster starts to crow, and an owl answers it. From a house further up the lane a dog barks, and the smell of mint is sharp in the damp, sprinkled air. She is weary with watching over them. She thinks about the night, before she told him to go, that Owen crawled up the hall in his boxer shorts, begging her to get him one last bottle of whiskey, the toilet floor wet from where he had missed the bowl. The bad memories are easier to tolerate, she decides.

In the supermarket next day, Marcus chooses Serrano ham and Coco Rocks; Abigail has watermelon and a family bar of Lindt chocolate; Florrie picks a whole cheese and some salt and vinegar crisps.

'Can we go into the old town?' says Abigail.

'Everything will melt,' says Kate.

Abigail goes away and comes back with a cool bag and two packs of ice cubes. 'Five euro,' she says. 'I'll pay.' And Kate looks at her strange daughter, whose brain is still problem-solving, despite the heat, despite everything.

'*Muy bien*,' she says. 'Okay.'

It's a random kind of booty they come away with: bananas and chorizo, olives and peanuts; nothing substantial; nothing her own mother would have approved of.

Outside, the heat hits them like an open oven door. They drive into the town and park the car, follow signs for *La Ciudad*, which the guidebook tells them is where they want to go. Almost before they realise it, they are on the bridge, the dizzying *Puente Nuevo* that spans the gorge between old town and new. The curved metal balustrades along the sides are crammed with sightseers standing on the brink, peering straight down thousands of feet to the bottom of the ravine below. Kate takes a picture, then asks a passer-by to take one of them all as they stand there, teetering on the edge.

'Daddy would have liked this,' says Marcus, and she knows that he's thought about it before he says it. It's a step he's made – the first sign of an opening, like the gap in the boards of the shutter in his room that sends a needle of sunlight across the wooden floor.

'Yes,' says Florrie, not thinking at all. 'He liked scaring us,' and Abigail shoots her a dagger of a look. Kate opens her mouth and then closes it again, and puts her arm across Florrie's shoulders. Marcus and Abigail had the best of him.

After Kate told Owen to go, he sobered up for a while. Then one day, when he dropped Florrie off from a party and she leant in the car window to ask about the weekend, she smelt drink on his breath. She would never stop him from seeing the children, she told him, but she would never allow them in the car with him again. There were other women by then. Abigail and Marcus remained tight-lipped but Florrie gave them marks out of ten: for presentation, cooking and 'up-for-the-craic'. A girl called Stacey scored highest. She taught them blackjack wearing a pink poncho, fried sausages that they ate with multi-coloured cocktail sticks and no vegetables. They didn't stay overnight. Kate told them that if they ever felt unsafe they were to phone her, right away, no matter what. It had cost Abigail a lot to make that call, and Kate would be indebted to her, forever. Stacey came to the funeral, shadow-eyed, shook Kate's hand wordlessly and kissed Florrie on the head, stumbled out over the graveyard in wooden clogs and painted, bare toes.

In the souvenir shops under the colonnade in the old town beyond the bridge, Marcus finds a slingshot and a kaleidoscope; Florrie chooses a tiny ceramic bead for each of her friends. Abigail buys a miniature shoe, a precious, jewelled, pointless thing, which the shopkeeper wraps and winds in red ribbon.

Back at the house they unpack their food and lunch on what they have bought. She has to keep an eye on Abigail who is always opening the shutters, letting in the midday sun. She doesn't like the dark, she says, and the light from the wall lamps is yellow and weak, a sad light. Still, says Kate, they have to try and keep the house cool; sleeping on the sprinkled lawn is not a sensible option.

There's a clock on the barometer in the hall – and one in the salon, and one on the dresser, and the little clock on her bedside table that stares at her in the night with its hard green eye – and none of them corresponds with another, nor with the time on her phone. It is a different hour in every room in the house.

They walk out under a lazy cloud of wasps to explore. In the garage there's a four-foot inflatable green crocodile, a lilo, two boogie boards and a ball. They take it in turns to blow them up and then scatter them across the pool, little floating islands for Florrie so she can swim from one to the other. Then they climb back into their sun-dried costumes and slip, one by one, into the water.

Next morning, when she wakes, there is a constellation of mosquito bites on her left foot, and one in the crook of her arm, near the good vein, the one from which, when she was pregnant, the nurse used to draw blood. This is unusual. When she used to holiday with Owen beside her, the mosquitoes never bothered her, but gorged themselves on him.

'It's my rich blood,' he used to say, raising his chin. 'The blood of chieftains.'

Downstairs, Abigail is standing in the garden facing the apple tree, her shoulders to the sun, reading a book. Above her, near the pool, the pleated fronds of the fan palm tree flap like a broken concertina. Florrie has taken the net that is meant for skimming dead insects off the surface of the pool and is running around on the grass, trying to catch a little white butterfly with brown-tipped wings. She finds Marcus at the front of the house, where the car is parked, catapulting walnuts over the rosemary hedge. She arranges breakfast for them on the table under the trellis of vines, where it is shady and cool and they sit down together. The sound of the wind in the trees, when it comes, is as welcome as running water.

She remembers Raquel and phones to thank her, to say that

they have arrived safely, that everything is beautiful.

'Thank God,' says Raquel. 'I've been thinking about you.'

Raquel and Owen met at university in Belfast long before Kate came on the scene. They were both studying English, Raquel as a foreign language. Kate was never jealous. Raquel's looks were very Spanish: long glossy hair, drowsy eyes, aquiline nose, but somehow maternal rather than sensual; there was never anything sexual between her and Owen. Now that Marcus had grown his hair skater-boy style, Raquel loved to wrap her fingers around his long blond curls; said they reminded her of Owen's when he was younger. She was a good friend to all of them.

Raquel has explained that when the house was renovated, some years back, the builders left part of the original stone work exposed in patches that, here and there, interrupt the whitewashed walls. To the right of the door inside the kitchen is a stone growing out into the room. It is the size of a man's head, chin jutting out, blank and defenceless. When Kate turns from the cracked ceramic sink to tell Florrie to drink more water, or ask Marcus to come in out of the sun, she thinks every time that a man is walking in, hands by his side, following his big benign chin in to the house.

When she has washed up the breakfast things, she walks out past the stone into the garden to properly stake out their territory. The property is enclosed by a man-height fence of chicken wire that she can see from beyond the garden door. She starts from the lime tree above the pool and walks the perimeter, past apricot and walnut trees, through the scent of rosemary and oregano and mint. Where the arc of the sprinkler stops, the earth is baked red and scorched with dry grass and thistles. Then, suddenly, there is a fig tree, and a frayed rope and a plank of wood splashed with bird droppings, and Abigail sitting on it, a character from a Victorian novel, pale and cool under complicated shadows.

'Do you want a push?' she asks, but Abigail shakes her head. In her lap is a notebook into the pages of which she is pressing leaves and flowers, scribing long secret notes in handwriting that belies her years. 'Fancy a dip?' Kate says.

In the pool, Marcus starts a game of water polo, and to begin with they splash each other ruthlessly with the ball. But after a while, they get better at judging the distances between each other; their highest score, without a drop is ten. Kate suddenly needs the toilet. She pulls herself up the metal steps from the pool and says, 'Two minutes. Marcus is in charge.' As soon as she is out of the water, she feels like her bladder is about to burst. She reaches round to the back of her neck to untie the halter of her swimsuit, but it is wet and knotted and when she is only halfway down the path, the compulsion to let go overwhelms her and she steps on to the lawn, showering it with pool water and pee. She slips out of her costume and walks back to the shower at the pool head. Then she hears Abigail's voice shouting, 'Marcus! Marcus!' and when she gets there, he is under the inflatable, his hair caught in a Velcro strip. She is in and has him by the neck, tearing the hair out of his head, hauling him clear, him choking and burping up water, and then they are all at the side, holding on, crying every one of them, gasping for breath.

'Mammo,' says Florrie when they've all recovered. 'You're naked!'

In the night she wakes in the sure knowledge that there is someone in the room; a deeper pooling of shadow at the foot of the bed, hands on the sheet, groping their way towards her head.

'Mammo,' says Abigail, 'the lights have all gone out.'

Together they go hand in hand down the stairs to the kitchen dresser for candles and matches. She finds a globe on the shelf, pushes the lighted candle into the holder, brings Abigail back to her room and puts the light down on the floor in the hall. She takes up vigil on her daughter's bed, her back against the worm-holed headboard, until Abigail's eyes close, and in her head she walks them through a day without electricity. When the sunlight begins to glow like an ember behind the shutter, she blows out the candle and climbs back into her own bed.

Marcus has found the fuse box by the front door, and all that's happened is that the trip has gone. They need more water and more bread so they go into Ronda and have a walk around. Marcus wants to see one of the churches that has been converted from a mosque, and the guidebook sends them to the old town, to *Iglesia de Santa María La Mayor*. Just inside is an exposed stone arch with Arabic inscriptions. Abigail is mesmerised by the expressions on the faces of the statues, none of them down-turned like in the churches at home, but all of them looking up or straight ahead exultant, or defiant. Marcus goes straight to the crypt, looking for bones. Kate pays one euro for a sturdy red plastic holder and candle; the man at the desk hands Florrie a lighter, and they put it in the candelabra by the door, and say a prayer of thanks to whoever it is that's watching over them.

In the garden at *Finca Los Nogales*, a two-way line of ants is

marching, one towards the clump of chives and oregano, each
carrying a crumb from the magdalenas the family has had at
lunch, the other line heading south, empty-mouthed, to gather
up the rest. Kate is lying on the sun lounger, her head in the
shade of the house, her long white feet stretched out in the sun.
Florrie has a biro and is joining up Kate's mosquito bites. 'Look
Mammo,' she says, 'the mossies left you a crown,' and there it
is – a crooked, drunken thing, but a crown nonetheless, of the
kind you might see on a storybook frog. From here she can hear
the black pods of the dry broom crackle and burst in the heat,
the noisy scattering of seed. Abigail is collecting, still. Kate can
hear the crunch of her feet over the walnuts and dry leaves. She
watches her pluck an unripe olive, polish it to a bright green
bullet on her tee shirt, slip it into the band of her skirt. At the
gap in the rosemary hedge, Marcus is building two small cairns
out of stones he has gathered from the garden. She can feel them
all stop and, together, listen for the sound of the rattling train
that starts like a promise in the east and stutters past. An apple
drops from the tree; the pine nuts are taking their own time to
brown; there is healing going on, quietly.

The evening that Abigail had rung her, Kate was flicking
through the channels, looking for the news, putting in time until
she went to collect them.

'Mammo,' Abigail said. 'Daddy says he's taking us to the
cinema.' There was a crack in her voice that needed no
explaining.

Kate lifted her keys and drove straight to the flat. The children
were already in Owen's car, Abigail's pale face peering through
the back windscreen. She opened both doors and marshalled
them out; she could smell the alcohol even from that distance.

She never broke breath to him again.

Now, in the garden, Florrie says, 'Can we go out for dinner, Mammo? To celebrate the light coming back on?'

'*Sí*,' says Kate.

She puts Florrie in the bath under the eaves and Florrie wants the shutter open so she can count the rainbows in the bubbles. She smells of chlorine and peach-scented sun cream, and there is a little mark on her ear where the sun has caught her. The flow of water dwindles as Abigail turns on the shower downstairs. She leaves Florrie to soak and goes to pick something out of the cobwebbed wardrobe.

She has been wearing the same blue ankle-length skirt for three days. None of the mirrors in the house show more than her head and shoulders. Every morning she wakes, her hair behind her right ear is curled out like a goose wing. It gives her a lopsided look, like only part of her knows where she is going. She unzips her make-up bag but her lipstick and eyeliner have softened in the heat. There is nothing sharp about the reflection that looks back at her. She shakes the folds out of some linen trousers and a loose white shirt and pulls them on, then stands on the toilet seat. But from there all she can see is her right leg. She asks Abigail's advice.

'Too much white,' says Abigail. She hands her a strappy lilac top and a pair of heeled sandals.

'I can't drive in those.'

'Put them on when we get there. Otherwise you'll look like you're out in your pyjamas.'

She slips her feet into her espadrilles, the sandals into the neck of her bag.

At the restaurant at the crossroads, the one that Raquel has recommended, there is nothing on the menu that any of the children want to eat. She sends the waiter away twice.

'What's in the kid stew, Mammo?' asks Florrie.

'Kid!' chime Marcus and Abigail together, and Florrie squeals.

The waiter brings what looks like a giant chicken goujon to the people at the table beside them.

Kate takes a deep breath and points: '*Cuatro, por favor,*' she says, '*con patatas fritas.*'

A woman sharing tapas with a man at a barrel-table stares languidly at Kate's white shoulders, at her pink-faced children, at the biro tattoo on her sandaled foot. In the road below, two boys go past carrying a mattress on their heads; and then four horses pass, each of the riders with reflective bands on their arms. They can see the lights flashing red long after the sound of the horses' hooves has gone. When the food comes, it is deliciously salty and they wash it down with water and Coke, and dab at the dark vinegar on their plates and suck it off their fingers. The bats begin to swoop from roof to roof. Kate is thinking of the night that Owen's car went off the road, the way the metal wrapped itself around the tree, almost lovingly, the way the indicator light went on blinking, off and on. 'More than four times the legal limit,' said the coroner. 'Death was almost instant.'

'Can horses see in the dark?' says Florrie.

In Andalusia, night drops down suddenly, like a stone.

It is their last full day and it is full of the sense of leaving. In the salon Kate lies down with her cheek to the cool ceramic tiles, gazes at the dust under the wicker sofa.

'What are you doing, Mammo?' asks Florrie.

'Just checking we haven't left anything,' she says.

'We have to leave something,' says Florrie. 'Everyone else has.'

She strips the sheets off the bed and tugs the mattress up to see if anything has fallen down. There is a pair of white knickers, twisted into a knot, kicked off in a hurry. They are not hers. She is happy to think that someone had a good time here; glad she didn't find them until now.

Florrie comes in and says she's found a snail tree. 'Like the pineapple tree?' asks Marcus, but they all go to look. Sure enough, there is a walnut tree in the garden whose trunk is covered in clusters of tiny white shells, like jewels, and all along the branches and clinging to the buds, and they do look like they are growing, strange hard fruit, their small backs a helix, ripe for picking.

Kate says, 'Today's the day we eat and drink everything that's left.'

'Like in *The Tiger Who Came to Tea*?' says Florrie, and Kate says, exactly like that. So they have marshmallows and chocolate and fizzy orange and dried apricots and cheese. There is an unopened packet of ham in the fridge that Florrie wants to bring home.

'It wouldn't travel well,' says Kate. 'We'll leave it for José.'

'What if he doesn't come?' says Florrie.

'It's Tuesday tomorrow. It's his day for the garden.'

'What if he doesn't come in the house?'

'We'll leave him a note.'

So Abigail tears a page out of her collecting book and they write in big letters, 'José' and then, '*Gracias. Jamón en el frigorífico.*' They melt a candle over an olive dish and use the wax to stick the note to the garden door.

'What if the sun melts it and it blows away?' says Florrie.

'It won't,' says Abigail, 'it just won't.'

Kate walks through the gap in the rosemary hedge, through a cobweb and the smell of cats' pee, to look at the new moon, and she rises a white moth out of the garden.

That night none of them wakes.

On the last morning, they walk out of the house, the four of them – Kate with her legs covered in bites; Marcus with a bellyful of pool water; Florrie with a sunburnt ear; Abigail with her heart a little melted – each of them marked by the place. They're all in the car when Abigail says, 'One minute.' She jumps out and runs down the garden, comes back and says, 'Close your eyes,' and presses something into the palm of Kate's hand. When Kate looks it is a walnut, a blind blunt-nosed, pock-marked thing, as dry and light as a heart can sometimes be.

'Alright,' she says. 'Are we ready?'

'*Sí*,' the children all say together, and they go.

Islander

I'm on the train, travelling towards the thing that is going to happen. I'm riding the jointed rooms of jolting metal that make up the train between the coast and the city. I'm sitting, one leg crossed over the other (you have to cross your legs quickly, before the person who might sit down opposite gets a chance to cross theirs) and I'm at the window, my rucksack safeguarding the seat next to the aisle. All I want to do is travel, shelve all decisions, let the train take responsibility for moving me.

The train is carrying me away. It is damp October and this is what I see. On the black tarmac of the platform is an impossible jigsaw of red and yellow leaves. The houses all have their backs to us; the entire population is facing the other way. I'm thinking that the people whose houses back on to railway lines don't travel by train and that if they did, they would remove the bottles from their windowsills, upright their overturned flower pots, clean up their back yards. They are exposing much more of their jumbled lives than they realise. At a railway crossing a small boy in the back of a white car waits without excitement for the train to pass. We plunge on, raising rooks off power lines, blowing our tuneless horn. A single blackthorn in an open field throws a short shadow: a fairy tree. Pulling the grass out of the earth with its yellow teeth is a black goat.

The train slows. My nerves tingle. This is it. Here comes the thing that is going to happen. It's a girl, my age, on the platform at a little-used halt, stepping in, carrying a story. She has a rucksack on her back. She walks towards me up the aisle of the still-moving almost-empty carriage and slides into the seat opposite mine. Impossibly, she crosses her legs. She throws a smile, I catch it; we both look out the window. In the darkening air outside, our eyes meet in the glass, somewhere near Balnamore, over the fairy tree where the black goat is grazing. And this is what she tells me with her eyes.

It was the start of the trip we'd promised ourselves, me and the girls, the one thing that had bolstered us up through all those weeks of Molière and Proust. Finals: the very word was enough to strike fear into the heart of every one of us. 'Your day of reckoning'll come, Sarah,' my father was fond of saying, and here it was. Ten days of reckoning to be precise; ten days with the smell of newly-cut grass in our noses, trying to ignore the sudden sunshine on the dusty walk to the Whitla Hall. Ten days of being bleary-eyed from lack of sleep and greasy-haired from lack of washing, wearing the first sloughed-off tee shirt we'd found on the floor that morning. And our promise to ourselves, driving our footsteps, that as soon as the last of us had put down the last pen on the last paper of the last exam, the others would be waiting outside, bags packed, ready to go. Corsica, Sardinia, Capri: these were the names we whispered to each other when our heads pounded with dates and lines; Elba, Sicily, Ischia. We would find work in cafés and restaurants, we would swim in the warm sea, sleep on the beach, live off goat's cheese and olives, breathe salt air. The trip was my idea, of course.

'Maybe it's because you're an only child,' my father said once, 'this thing for islands – a desire to be marooned.'

And it was my idea to start on Rathlin, an ironic farewell to childhood summers under dripping canvas, seals in the bay, pebbles on the beach, shallow grassy lakes where you could lose yourself.

The one bar on the island was crammed full of people, spilling out into the night. From the rough wooden tables that overlooked the harbour outside, guitar music drifted in and out and a voice rose in song, carried by the breeze over the Moyle. It wasn't long before I spotted Charlie. Wherever I was in the room, whenever I lifted my eyes, he was there, smiling, hand curled around a pint glass. He walked with me to the hostel, with the cows lowing behind the hedges. As we left the lights of the pub behind and climbed the path that sloped gently into the dark hillside, I felt the breath of the place. One mile wide, narrow enough to keep one edge of it always in your sights, you can never shake off the feeling that you're stranded. An island makes you exempt; it gives you permission to be someone else. I sneaked a look at Charlie, and the torch of light from Rue Point swept across the green island and touched my bare face and then his. When he felt for and found my hand, it was like a choice he'd made.

He teased me about my background, called me 'Daddy's little girl'. He was the youngest of seven sons, his father lost in a capsized boat when he was just eight years old. I couldn't get my head around it, the idea of sharing your parents with six other people, all of whom had an equal claim. I told him about my mother, about what I knew of her, and my twin sister, both dead the day I was born. I always said I'd end up with a

Corsican or a Sicilian, and here I was with an islander from six miles off my own coast. I tried to explain it to Charlie, the island feeling, the sense of being cut off and being released at the same time. He didn't understand. He'd moved away, learnt a trade, found work in a builder's yard; but he'd been born there, it was his familiar world, he hadn't come from somewhere else. I never made it to the Mediterranean.

Charlie said I should meet his family, so I made the trip. It was a bad night, September on the turn, not taking time to rain. The water bounced off the steep black road from the harbour, stair spindles in the car lights. I was nervous about meeting his mother and the rest of them, and about what it was we had to say. The smell of oil and wet chamois leather grabbed at my throat and I closed my eyes. I could hear the water scatter as he drove too fast through troughs of it. It was one of his games, trying to scare me. I gripped the seat. There was a sudden jerk as the tyres lost their hold; a sickening sideways motion as the car glided across the road. I opened my eyes to see the white trunk of a dead tree leer out from the edge of a field, a broad, pale spade of a face in the dark. It's the last thing I remember. Charlie, no seat belt, ended up face-down in a flooded ditch. They weren't able to save him: my father's words when I woke in the mainland hospital.

I said, 'Save him from what?' Nothing made any sense.

I made it to Charlie's mother's house in the end, my father with me, picking our steps through the farmyard mud at the gable of the house. In the kitchen window, women moved in and out of a yellow rectangle of light, elbowing for space among sugar bowls and biscuit tins, making and carrying pots of tea. There was a hush when we entered by the front door and made our way up the hallway, searching unknown faces for signs of grief. A man said, 'He's just through there, into your right.' I half expected to find him in the armchair, legs hanging over the side, a mug of tea in his hand.

Charlie lay in the coffin by the drawn window, his fingers intertwined, two tiny nicks like razor cuts in the side of his head. I tried to remember a prayer but nothing came. I turned and caught the eyes of a woman who was seated in a chair by the side of the room. Charlie's mother had been watching me, and as I stepped away from the coffin, she stretched two age-marked hands towards me and took my bandaged wrists in hers. I looked into her lined face and saw the long road ahead of me.

'God bless you, daughter,' she said. A noise rose and stopped in my mouth for the woman I'd never know.

We sat in an emptied bedroom at the rear of the house, with thin china cups warming our hands. Women appeared and disappeared like spectres, clinking crockery. In another room, a man told a story about the time Charlie kept the hens in an old abandoned car at the bottom of the field. There was muted laughter – jokes about hatchbacks and wing mirrors, eggs in the glove compartment – before they all fell silent again. I could have pointed to the moment when their thoughts turned to the wreck of Charlie's car still lying in the ditch.

We left the wake house, the alien rituals. In the yard we were asked to pull in to allow other cars to make their way up the narrow lane. We sat and watched the smoke from the men's cigarettes rise up into the night.

My father said, 'They told me, Sarah, in the hospital. What are you going to do?'

How was I supposed to know? How come I was supposed to

have all the answers?

'I wish your mother was here,' he said, and he turned the key in the ignition.

We didn't speak the whole way back. We walked blinking into the guesthouse kitchen, one behind the other, and brushed the mud from the field off our shoes. I went to the back door and stood on the step for a long while, looking into the night. A pale sickle of a moon hung low in the cleared sky. What would my mother say to me, if she were here, or my sister? There were times like this when I felt them near me, thought I could sense them looking in at me in the doorway, the way I had looked in at the women in the wake house kitchen.

The train is cutting under, over, through. We rush past the discarded Pierrot hats of traffic cones, banded red and white; unearthed drains and pipes; glimpses of the underside of things. In the near-stripped trees I can see the dark clusters of abandoned nests. The grass is beaded with rain. A drift of smoke catches my nostrils from a man making his way back from the train toilet. He glances at me, at my bandaged arm. The seat across from me is empty.

The train is slowing now. We are almost there. A mist is coming down, catching on all the cobwebbed lives that have lain hidden in the day. I have an image now in my mind of the people on the island in Charlie's mother's house, shuffling through the whole of the long night and into the sunless dawn. It seems to me that they might go on forever, shoring each other up with stories, clattering about with tins and trays, busy putting off the burial. I put my hand on my belly. There is a shimmer of mirrored movement from the window. The girl is on the platform, looking in, mouth moving, saying something. I feel a tiny limb waken and push love into the cup of my hand.

'We do what we can,' she is saying, 'they with their stories and their clatter, and us with ours. We carry the living, and we do whatever it takes to wake the dead.'

What I Was Left

I am in the habit of collecting skies, and this one is a keeper. August evening on a Siena hillside, a sky that would put you in mind of King Louis's court, all swathes of blue silk, piled powdered wigs and, towards the west, a hint of blushing flesh. Above where I sit on the villa balcony, the clouds are beginning to darken, move faster, already intent on somewhere else. Dusty pinecones, *limoncello* sharp on the tongue, and peace, I am thinking, there is definitely peace. I breathe it all in, twice: once for me, and once for... well, let's not get ahead of ourselves.

Florence was too much for me: the *Duomo* shimmering like a white-iced cake; the *gelaterie* with their cracked coconut shells, as if some monstrous bird had just emerged; counters bearing watermelon, translucent pink, dark-seeded. I don't know how the Florentines can stand it, how they can go about their business every day amid all that sensory clamour, everything in the sunlight too bright, too pungent, too close. Who wouldn't feel cowed by the *campanile*; the blinding façade of *Santa Croce*, all that gilt and splendour so casually laid on? After I walked out of the Convention Centre, after I'd seen my mother for the first time in forty years, I hurried through the streets, head bowed, back to my own hotel, craving a shuttered room. I knew I was going to need a sky.

As the doors of the hotel lift met, I felt the now-familiar shiver snake up my spine, the sweat gather on my forehead, the tips of my fingers grow numb, the metallic taste on the lips, the ammoniac smell in the nose. It had been a while since I'd needed one of my skies, and for a moment I couldn't summon one up. Then I found one: the sky from Aunt Heather's room in the nursing home nearly six months before. The manager of the home had phoned me, said Aunt Heather was agitated, had grown confused.

'She's looking around all the time,' the nurse said when I got there, 'searching faces. She keeps asking for you.'

'Aunt Heather,' I said. 'It's Laurie.'

She looked at me then, with her serious grey eyes. Her legs under the bedclothes stilled.

'What's the day doing?' she said. 'Laurie, tell me the day.'

So I told her, the way she used to tell me. An Irish February on the northern coast, the sun a soft bulb, a great day for shadows, the strand glassy, mirroring blue. Two skies: one stretching overhead, entirely whole; the other scattered, lying about the sand in fragments of captured water, the broken passage of gulls reflected from one still pool to the next; the dunes shadowed and heatless, white-tipped waves picked out in the cold sun, Mussenden Temple a black mole on the headland of Benevenagh.

My great-aunt Heather brought me up. I was born, unplanned, when my mother Rosa was sixteen. She disappeared a few weeks later. I had a catalogue in my head of rare facts about Rosa: at sixteen she wore her hair down to her waist; she got herself expelled from school for smoking; she liked to swim at Port-na-Happle at night. I thought of her as fearless. Aunt

Heather didn't talk much about her, talked more about her sister, my grandmother Alice, who died of tuberculosis in the fifties when my mother was just a child. She said I looked more like my grandmother: tall, light-haired, angular. Not graceful, then, was what I thought: elbowed, awkward, misfitting. 'And you're strong like her,' she used to say. 'She was never easy turned.'

Aunt Heather was delighted when I became a nursery school teacher. And I felt safe, surrounded by children, with no obligation to bring any of them home. I've never had any desire for a family, to have my body invaded by a child. I don't think I have the capacity. Not that I've had much success with men. Physical intimacy makes me claustrophobic – like a pillow over my mouth and nose, like trying to breathe through feathers.

In the nursing home on the hill overlooking the strand, I turned back from the window and Aunt Heather smiled, motioned me nearer the bed. 'You're not easily spooked, Laurie, are you?'

I stared at her. 'What do you mean?' I said.

'I never wanted you to be on your own.'

'I'm not on my own. I've got you.'

She closed her eyes then, sank back on the pillow, began to breathe easy. 'Stay with me, Laurie, promise?'

'Of course I'll stay.'

I returned to the window, looked down at the strand, put one hand over my ear like we used to when we found a shell, felt the blood pumping in my eardrum. The sound of the sea, Aunt Heather's breathing, the sound of the sea, off and on. Then Aunt Heather's breathing grew louder and it became another sound, like when you untie the mouth of a balloon that's been up for days, and that sound hung in the air above her bed. And then it moved away, towards the window, to where I was standing, to where I breathed it in. And after that, mine was the only breath in the room.

Next I felt the panic rise in me, felt a sensation in my chest like the beat of a wing, smelt wood smoke and disinfectant, tasted blood on my lips, and the room tilted and the sea went where the sky should have been, and then it was dark.

After Aunt Heather died, I went to the doctor about the constriction in my chest, the whispered breathing. He said it was unusual for asthma to begin so late in life. He asked me to describe how it felt. 'Like someone lying on top of me,' I said and he nodded and wrote a prescription for an inhaler. I threw out all the feather pillows and duvets and Aunt Heather's red-patterned rug, the one that had come from the old house. The doctor said the attacks might pass with time. But I hadn't been telling the whole truth when I described the sensation to him. It was more like a knee on my chest; it was like a fist in my mouth; it was like someone trying to climb inside me. I taught myself how to breathe when the panic came. I learned how to collect skies.

I was going through Aunt Heather's belongings and I found a tight bundle of letters and photos, circled in a crumbling rubber band, on which she had written, 'Laurie's things'. In the bundle were some photographs of me as a baby, and one of my mother in a plaid mini skirt, taken the summer before I was born. The last in the bundle was a postcard dated November 1966. It was a black-and-white photo of an avenue in the Boboli Gardens, a place that put me in mind of the Frosses near home where the trees lean over and kiss above the road. On the back was a forty-lira stamp. It was addressed to Aunt Heather and it read: 'I'm sorry. I can't do it. Please look after Laurie. I'm in Florence, helping out after the flood. I love you both, Rosa.'

I researched the 'Mud Angels' in the library, the flocks of Beat Generation youngsters who'd made their way to Florence when the Arno burst its banks in '66. There were pictures of them, knee deep in mud, working sometimes by candlelight to clear away muck and debris, scrape oil off canvasses, drag books out of the slime of the *Biblioteca Nazionale*. How was I supposed to feel about that? Proud? That my mother had felt it her duty to salvage art for the legacy of generations to come, but had felt nothing at all for me? While I was still there reading the librarian handed me an article. 'I thought you might be interested in this,' she said.

Legambiente, an Italian environmental organisation, was promoting a reunion of *gli angeli del fango* forty years after the event. They were calling for the original mud angels to come. They had collated a list of names. I felt like I held my heart in my hand as I scanned down through the column of foreign angels: Shannon, Sharwood, Shatner, Shaw. Rosa Shaw. My mother.

The event was well organised. The walls of the foyer of the Hotel Bel Arno were lined with grainy black-and-whites: a dead cow being winched out of the Arno; a boy in military uniform wiping mud from the face of a crucifix; a suited man, his face bereft, filling a wine carafe at the Fountain of Neptune.

'Rosa!' I heard someone cry, and I turned to see two women collide in an embrace, the taller of the two, in cool linen, low-heeled gold sandals, her brown hair highlighted. There was a flurry of hugs, delighted cries, a standing back to appraise. 'My God, Carla, you look exactly the same!' Mid-fifties, the trace of an Irish accent still, and the badge on her lapel: Rosa Shaw Ferrara. 'Come and meet Antonio,' and she led the woman to a dark-suited man. They began to speak in rapid Italian. In answer to a question, my mother took a wallet from her bag: '*Franco e Roberto*,' she said and the other woman cooed.

So this was her. She had adopted Italy; this was her husband, these smiling pictured faces her family. I could have walked up to her then, introduced myself, the abandoned daughter. But what would have been the use of that? Aunt Heather had been mother enough for me.

Maybe because I'd borrowed her sky, maybe because I'd seen Rosa, Aunt Heather came into my dream that night and she told me a serious thing. She told me she'd given me a life to carry. She told me that the skies wouldn't always work. I was answering her, asking what she meant, but my heart was pounding in my chest and I woke up to the sound of my own voice, thick with sleep, making no sense.

On the balcony in Monticiano, as the fireflies spark in the dusk under the pines and the shiver begins to snake again up my spine, I put the glass of *limoncello* to my lips and swallow hard. I am considering what has been offered to me, what Aunt Heather breathed into me with her last breath. And now I have two lives to live: my own and hers. She is here still; she could not leave me. She has stayed to live life second-hand for as long as I can carry her.

The Bells Were Ringing Out

Nuala O'Reilly was between Hislop's and the butcher's when she forgot who she was. She didn't do any of the usual things a person does when they realise they've forgotten something. She didn't stop in the street and swear under her breath, or turn on her heel and go back the way she'd come, or search in her bag to see if the thing she thought she'd forgotten was there after all. She kept on moving. Her feet seemed to know where to go. When she reached the glass-paned door of the butcher's shop, she glanced at the face that looked back at her. Cropped, dirty blonde hair, green eyes, a thick grey scarf at her throat. The nails of the hand on the door were free of polish, a little inky, broken in places, a single gold band on the ring finger. The air was sharp, tinny Christmas music filtering over the tannoy on the street. She pushed the door and went in.

The man behind the counter smiled at her and said, 'What can I get you?' and she noticed that all his vowels, when he spoke them, had colours as well as shapes and hung in the air like errant musical notes between them. The 'u' lasted longest, a pot of deep blue ink.

'Two chicken fillets,' she said without hesitation and watched as the 'o' bounced off the counter, a white balloon. The 'i' was a dark tie with purple dots and the 'e' was an eye, squinting in a sun-filled photograph. It was a little distracting. The butcher didn't seem to notice.

'Will that be all?' he said and the 'a' was a green plastic watering can with the handle reaching over the top.

She nodded. In the leather satchel that hung across her shoulder she found a black purse, stuffed with receipts, a twenty-pound note. She paid the butcher and left the shop and looked down at her feet, walking. A pair of short brown leather boots, a little weather-stained, jeans, a waist-length quilted jacket. Something warm underneath, a sweater, maybe. She walked down the street and into a coffee shop where she asked for a pot of earl grey tea and the vowels went skipping over the newspaper on the counter that declared it to be Tuesday, the ninth of December. In her head, a woman's voice said, 'Tuesday is tangerine; pitted, like the orange,' and the words left a moss-green pain in her chest. She took a seat by the window, removed the lid from the teapot, breathed in the perfume of the tea and it eased a little the throbbing that had begun in her head. Then she opened the bag.

Nearly all the receipts were dated the previous day, one from an art suppliers for ink and cutters, one from a garage forecourt shop, thirty pounds of unleaded, apples, bread, milk. She found a ticket for a car park in Railway Place with the time printed (09:17) and an online receipt for a return train journey for Belfast, both with today's date. She saw herself at the wheel of a car, a railway barrier, a train pulling out. At the bottom of the bag, a set of three keys; in a side pocket a credit card with a name: Nuala O'Reilly. She said the name aloud and all the vowels reeled, briefly, in the steam above the teapot. She held the keys in her hand: a thick black one bearing a Ford emblem; a single, silver Yale lock key; a bronze skeleton key for an old-fashioned lock. She drank her cooled tea and wondered, mildly, if there was anyone waiting for her, if she was expected. She unzipped her jacket pocket, a crumpled tissue with make-up on it, strawberry lip salve, a mobile phone. She scrolled down through the texts. Someone called James Harty wanted to know if she could drop the prints off before Christmas. A text from Sam read: 'Delivered safely. Have a good day.' A saved phone message from Lizzie said the company would put her up at The Girona on Monday night. She listened to the voice in the message three times and the same voice in her head said Monday was a blue moon. Sam, Lizzie, people with no surnames. The time on the phone said 10:39.

She followed the signs to the railway station. In the car park she walked up to every Ford model and squeezed the unlock button on the thick black key. After nine or so, there was a click, a dark blue Ford Focus with a National Trust sticker. The car boot contained four framed prints, book-sized, bubble-wrapped, and a purple and blue checked blanket. Inside, on the driver's side, a sprinkling of sand round the pedals; in the back (her heart shifted), a child's booster seat. In her head she saw a boy of three or four holding a crayoned drawing, saying he'd got a star and the green watering can went spinning.

In the glove compartment she found a satnav. To the question 'Where to?' she answered 'Home' and a woman's voice, gentle and persuasive, guided her out of the car park, all her vowels waltzing, through the town and down along the water for two or three miles until the river widened and the road turned away. The voice took her to a driveway in a seaside town, to a pebble-dashed semi with a red chimney pot, gulls screeching overhead.

She got out with the leather satchel and the plastic bag, and she turned the silver key in the lock of a blue-painted door and pushed it open.

The house smelled of vanilla. On the black tiles in the porch were two pairs of welly boots caked in sand, one pair about the same size as the boots she was wearing, the other much smaller and striped with colour. She walked through the hall, past a door to her left, under an arch to a modest-sized kitchen. All the walls were the colour of oatmeal, the floor a rich engrained oak. There was a table and chairs, and a heavy mahogany sideboard with framed photographs, one of a dark-haired man, smiling, holding a baby in his arms. In the photo he was wearing a light blue tee shirt, but she suddenly saw him in a dark suit and tie with the boy by the hand saying, 'You'll miss your train. I'll drop him off – pick him up as well,' and the vowels began to lurch around the kitchen, spotted ties and ink pots, watering cans and balloons in green and purple, navy and white. In another photograph, she recognised herself in pale chiffon with another woman, a little taller, in dark silk, their arms hooked through, smiling out, the two of them, matching flowers in their hair. The other woman had the same colour eyes but a different shape from her own, the shape of the 'e' when she heard it out loud.

'Friday's a good day to get married,' the woman's voice said. 'It's a conker, glossy brown, solid.'

Lizzie, her sister, her voice, her eyes. Something rose in her, something she knew, something sudden and unwelcome, a colour that didn't have a shape yet because she couldn't let it, moss green, growing.

A fruit bowl on the island counter held a cut lime and she saw herself there at the sink facing the room, filling ice into three tall glasses, mixing gin, the bite of lime juice at a quicked nail, the chink of cut glass, and laughter. The sink was empty, ringed with coffee grounds, a child's hand-painted mug on the drainer, a bunch of yellow tulips in the clear bell of a vase. By the back door, a green plastic watering can. She put the chicken in the fridge.

In the living room off the hall to her right there was a TV, a pale corded suite, prints on the walls. Upstairs, a double room and a single, the walls of the second papered with the alphabet, a child's drawings, a small bed. The third room, at the front of the house, was locked. She reached into the bag that was still across her shoulder, took out the skeleton key and put it in the lock, turned the Bakelite doorknob and walked inside. A bench ran beneath the window the full length of the wall and on it stood a cast iron hand press with two red arms that reached down and around the plates and a black metal crossbar, like a giant corkscrew on top. The surfaces were strewn with pots of coloured ink, tubes of paint, wooden-handled tools, loose blades and brushes. From a box at one end spilled rolls of wallpaper, ink-stained lace, coloured tissue, corrugated cardboard. Sections of dark lino softened on the radiator. On the wall to the left of the window was a photograph of the boy's face and underneath, sheet after printed sheet of the same face taken at the same angle, some in reverse, in green and purple and red and deep blue, all of them failing to capture him, the turn of his head, the tilt of his chin, until the last sheet she picked up. A few dark strokes in a white space, the curve of an eyebrow, the flare of a nostril, a lock of hair, a shadow under his lip, the beauty of him. She could feel the weight of the gouge in her hand, the give in the lino, the contours of ink on her fingertips. She left the studio, relocked the door, went into the child's room and lay down on the bed; and the smell of the pillow was a ball of love and she closed her eyes.

When she woke, the hands of the alphabet clock on the little bedside table pointed to five and she got up and went back down to the kitchen. In the cupboard by the fridge she found a bag of potatoes and she emptied it into the sink and began to peel them, one by one. Then there was the scrape of a key in the door, and a man's footstep, and a child's voice and the man shouted, 'Hello?' and the boy shouted 'Mummy!' and came running in, right into her arms and she held him until he wriggled free. 'Did you get me anything?' the boy said and she shook her head and he moaned a fake moan.

'I didn't think you'd be back yet,' the man in the dark suit said.

The boy tugged her hand. 'Can I watch TV?' She nodded and watched him run off.

'Tired?' the man said, a dark tie at his throat.

'Yes.'

'That's the big city for you,' and he took off the tie, rolled it up, shoved it in the pocket of his jacket. 'Need any help?'

She shook her head, a taste rising at the back of her throat, green and bitter. He turned and dropped his keys on the sideboard, began to hum something she could almost put words to, filling the kitchen with swirling watering cans, and balloons and spotted ties and pots of ink and smiling eyes from old photographs. Something she'd heard, thin and tinny, out in the street. 'That song's been in my head all day,' he said.

She was turning on the hot tap, running water over the scraped potatoes, looking at his back. And then she was in the town again, between Hislop's and the butcher's. She had missed her train, had decided not to go to Belfast, could deliver the prints another time. She'd been in to look at the shoes in Hislop's and seen nothing to better the boots she was wearing, and she'd decided to cook something hearty for dinner and she was walking out and there was a boy, a little younger than her's, clutching the string of a white balloon, and a gust of wind had caught it and he had lost his grip and the balloon had risen up and away from him, and he shouted and cried and his mother jumped up but it was out of reach for her already and the wind carried it across the street and it drifted on up past Hislop's and the chemist, almost as far as the hotel, where a man in a suit emerged from the side door and a woman called after him, the woman with the tangerine, blue moon, conkers voice, the woman with the eyes of the woman in the photograph, and she handed him something and he took it and smiled and they didn't touch at all, apart from that, or speak at all, apart from that, and he put the tie around his neck and left.

In the kitchen he says, 'Nuala?' and she says 'What?' and he's looking at the tap; and she looks down at her scalded hands and it's only now that he's said her name that the pain has a shape as well as a feel: a hand in a dark pool, rank with weeds, a smell that fills your nose and lingers.

The Recipe

It's a Friday evening, late February, condensation running down the kitchen windows. Deirdre has dropped in and is leaning against the worktop while I cook. She has had an encounter in the supermarket. I press down the switch on the kettle.

Deirdre Steele is what I call 'brittle'. She drums her bony, ringless fingers on the granite while she waits for the water to boil. There's not a scrap of spare flesh on her. She hasn't been in my department for very long, is generally considered cold at school, doesn't give much away. I happen to know that her form class call her 'Steeleknickers'. But her sense of humour appeals to me: her caustic remarks about the Principal's built-up shoes; her take on the secretary's ratty hair extensions. She's the bitch I'd sometimes like to be. Right now, though, I could do without her: Harry's just rung to say his thankless sister is coming for dinner and multi-tasking is not my thing.

I have my head in the larder trying to remember what it is my sister-in-law doesn't eat now – pasta, is it? or rice? – when I hear Deirdre say, over the rumble of the kettle, '... her father used to steal spades.'

'Whose father?' I say from the cupboard.

'Cecilia's. Old Denny Johnson – he used to steal spades.'

'Spades?' I say in a too-high voice, wondering who Cecilia is.

I don't cook well even when I'm not being distracted.

'Nothing else,' she goes on, 'not picks or shovels or rakes, just spades. Everybody knew about it. He kept them in the shed at the bottom of the garden. Any time any of the neighbours missed a spade, they'd walk over to the house, knock on the door and say, "Denny, would you open the shed?"'

The olive oil is beginning to smoke and I push the pan off the hob. I spoon coffee into a mug, my eyes beginning to water from the burnt oil.

I say: 'Did nobody ever report him?' And still I have no idea who we're talking about.

'Why would they?' she says. 'It was harmless. Denny would lift the key from below the holy water font in the hall, walk down the garden, open the shed and the neighbour would go in, pick out their spade, say, "Cheers Denny", like he was lending it to them, and Denny would lock the shed on all the other stolen spades.'

'It seems odd,' I say, which is not adequate, but I'm thinking about the oil and whether I should throw it out and start over again. I hand her the mug of coffee, black, unsweetened.

She takes a sip and says: 'Yes. And that's what really annoys her.'

'Well, it would,' I say.

'Not that he did it,' says Deirdre.

'No?'

'It's that I *know* about it. It annoys her to see me at all because seeing me reminds her of her family, *and* of the spades, *and* of Grangemore. She'd like to forget that that's where she came from.'

'I see,' I say, which is true. I do see, but I don't know why she's telling me this.

I've decided not to risk the oil and I'm pouring it down the drain and wiping the pan with kitchen paper and putting fresh oil in, with butter this time for a bit of added flavour. And I'm thinking I can make something stew-like with chicken that we can eat with pasta or rice, or potatoes, or bread even. I'll have Harry to listen to if I don't produce a carbohydrate of some description. And I gather myself and say: 'What did she say?'

Deirdre grunts, a noise I haven't heard her make before. 'You want to have seen her face when I came round the corner of the aisle. She had Mrs Givens – you know, who's married to the dentist – pinned up against the olives, and she's saying, "Oh yes, a country girl at heart," and you can see Mrs Givens thinking horses and gymkhanas which is what *she* wants her to think. Far from the country club was *she* reared! She's invented a whole fable about herself and when she caught sight of me she didn't know who to be. She turned tail and ran, straight into the discount aisle.'

This is the longest speech I've ever heard Deirdre make. She's clearly ruffled. Her face, beneath her sculpted dark bob, is pale. There's a little smudge of lipstick on her chemically whitened teeth. I'm peeling the paper skin off an onion and carefully I say: 'Did you blow her cover?'

'No,' says Deirdre. 'Not this time. But she'd better not come all Madam Butterfly with me or she'll get her comeuppance. They didn't get an inside toilet till she was six. She never had a stitch to wear that hadn't been round half a dozen of her cousins before her.'

I look at Deirdre's nails, at the French-manicured, toughened half moons that never seem to chip on the keyboard in school.

And I look at mine, chewed and ragged, smelling now of onion. Deirdre doesn't do chopping. Deirdre does microwave-ready meals-for-one. She seems to like it that way. I've never heard her mention a man. Jim Riley swore there was something between her and Sam Mulholland at the Christmas do: they shared a taxi home, dropped Jim off first. But Sam's a married man with two kids in college; he's only just made Head of Department. I can't see it. Not that she would tell me. Not that she would tell anyone.

'You knew her well, then?' I say.

'We were at primary school together.'

'And you lost touch?'

'You could say that. Where we lived, you didn't choose your friends. You just played with whoever was there: "kick-the-tin", "boys-after-the-girls". She was very good at conkers, I remember – smashed mine to a pulp.'

I'm trying to imagine Deirdre with a conker, but the image is too difficult to summon. I've got the onion in the pan and I'm pushing it around with a wooden spoon and there's something bothering me, something from further back.

'What did he do with them?' I say. 'The father. What did he do with all the spades?'

'He used them.'

'Was he a gardener?'

'He was a gravedigger. He was trying to get the best one for the job. He said a straight-sided grave was a great comfort to a grieving family. He was always looking for the perfect spade.'

I turn the heat down under the pan and say: 'Imagine if that was your job – digging holes in the earth to put dead people in.'

Deirdre's blue-black eyelashes flicker. 'Somebody has to do

it. And old Denny took pride in his work. He was a local historian, really. He was the only one who knew where people were buried, what was an unmarked grave and what was an empty plot, how many bodies there were in the ground. He used to say,' – Deirdre lowers her voice – '"I'm the biggest boss in the townland. I have three hundred men under me".'

I laugh, smash the flat end of a knife on to a garlic clove, scoop the mess in with the onion.

Deirdre stares into her cup. 'I never liked to see them open a grave,' she says. 'If it was a family plot, they'd often have to do that. And if the weather was wet, or the grave was in a bad place, on a bit of a slope, the sides could collapse, uncover a casket that was already there. Sometimes it would be broken, from the weight of all that earth, and the years it'd been down there. You never knew what you were going to see.'

I look at her. 'Did you spend a lot of time in the graveyard?'

Deirdre shrugs: 'There wasn't much to do. Even a burial was an event. The graveyard was a shortcut, if the weather was dry enough, between the houses and the shop.'

I start to scissor some chicken, am gripping a slippery fillet, nicking off fat and gristle, when she says, 'This one time, in the summer, bored out of our heads, we were messing about, a crowd of us on our way to buy sweets. We were at that stage when you're not really into boys, but you're desperate to impress them – to act like you're one of the gang. And we went through the graveyard and we could see that down towards the bottom end, under the yew tree, there was a mound of earth where the men had left a grave open – the diggers must have gone over to the Parochial House for a drink of tea. It was the part of the graveyard that they said was unconsecrated – where they used to put unbaptised babies, suicide victims. Somebody told me people were buried there that had died in drink. We went down to have a look. The side of the hole that Denny and the men had dug had collapsed a bit. We could see a little pine box with the side out of it, something white lying in the clay. We were all standing, lined around the edge, staring down at it. And after a minute Cecilia said, "I dare you, Deirdre, to jump in and see what it is!" and all the boys started chanting, "Dare or die! Dare or die!" and Cecilia said, "Go on, we'll help you get back out again." So I jumped in, right into the grave in my Moses sandals, and got down on my hunkers, and scraped back the earth, and it was the bones of a tiny hand, the smallest I'd ever seen. I leaned back against the wall of the grave, looked up at the dark faces of Cecilia and the boys, at the clouds going past slow above them, and I could smell the damp of the earth and for a second or two, no one spoke, everything seemed very still. I could see where the roots of the tree were coming through the grave, white where the men's spades had cut them clean, and I could feel the clay squeeze in between my toes. And then Cecilia – it was definitely her – picked up a clod of earth and threw it straight at me, and shouted "Sucker!" and ran. And the rest of them all ran after her and left me in the grave.'

Deirdre presses her finger into a line of crumbs on the worktop, scrapes them off with her thumbnail, picks them back up again.

I'm looking at her, scissors in hand. 'How did you get out?'

'I got a foothold high up on one of the roots but I couldn't hoist myself up. I knew the men wouldn't be away long. I knew I'd be killed if they got me there. I had to put my other foot on the coffin lid, where it still held solid. I managed to haul myself out on to my elbows. I felt the lid give way just as I pushed up. I didn't look back.'

'And Cecilia …?'

'I never spoke to her again. It's years since I saw her. She trained to be a nurse, did the classic – nabbed the first doctor she got a hold of, got pregnant, got married, job done! From council house to Victorian detached in one fell shag! Last time I saw her was at old Denny's funeral. It's a wonder she showed up at all. It must have cost her something to bring the doctor up Church Road.'

I consider the contents of the pan, wonder whether I should add tomatoes or olives, call the whole thing 'Tuscan rustic'. I'm still looking at it when something occurs to me.

'The grave,' I say, putting a lid on the pan, 'the father's grave. Do you think the sides were straight enough for him?'

Only a slight smile from Deirdre. 'They were,' she says, 'dead straight.'

She puts her cup down with a chink and reaches for her keys. She has to go, she says, she's only keeping me back, she'll see herself out.

Then she turns at the door and says: 'I won't be in on Monday. I have to go to England for a couple of days: a medical thing, routine. I've cleared it with Sam.' Her voice cracks a little. 'I'll be back by the end of the week.'

I stare at the pan. The dinner's a mess.

'Okay,' I say without turning my head, without looking her in the eye, and she pauses for just a second and then she leaves me, with the pan bubbling gently, and little wisps of steam escaping from under the lid.

Marked

I'm watching for old Mr Kenny. He has a different knot in his tie for every day of the week. Not always the same knot for the same day, but seven knots certainly, depending on his mood and never the same knot two days in a row. I have googled their names and when I'm stuck about something, I use them to help me make decisions. If he's wearing his Windsor, that's a definite 'No'; you don't mess with the Windsor.

I come to the library every day after school, weekends as well. They're used to me here. When I come in now, the staff barely raise their heads. Some days there are new people, Canadians mostly, looking for their family roots and they drink me in, but when they've had their fill they carry on, sifting through parish records, talking under their breath. Staring is addictive but it's tiring too. There's only so much of it you can do. Mr Kenny comes in to read the papers. He has a face like unrisen dough; it's pale and fleshy and he doesn't look well, but no one stares at him the way they stare at me. My face doesn't fit me at all. Some people think it's a joke, and it is in a way, but it's a bad one and that's a difficult thing to walk around with. The library is a good place to be.

My mum always said I wasn't the one with the problem, it was other people that were the trouble. I do get that, most of the time, but it's hard when no one sits beside you for lunch and you never get picked as a partner on school trips. Becca's my friend but strictly outside of school. We were at primary together. She comes round to our flat sometimes but in school she acts like she doesn't know me. She's explained it to me, how she can't sit with me, because then she'll have no friends as well. I understand. No one wants to hang out with the clown-face girl.

It was hard to go to the new school. It took a long time for people to get used to me. Now it's only the new intake I have to worry about. Every September I get 'Crusty!' from a few brave Year Eights and then they fall about laughing like they've just invented it. When I first came the older ones tried to outdo each other: 'I'll have fries with that, Ronald,' was a favourite for a while, but Clown Face is the one that has stuck. You can't be too clever when it comes to a nickname. The simple ones are the best.

Today, after Geography, when I went to the canteen for lunch, there was a text on my phone. It said, 'C U 2moro after school behind the mobiles,' and it was signed Neil Chambers. He was sitting behind me in class. He's nice-looking, like a shorter, blond-haired Robert Pattinson, but he never speaks to me. He hangs around with the skateboarding crowd down at the Crescent. I see them smoking sometimes behind the bus shelter. In the summer they go tombstoning off the harbour wall into the sea. They're quiet, watchful; not like the football guys – you hear *them* before you see them. Becca says she snogged Neil Chambers once and he tasted of chicken curry and it nearly turned her because she's vegetarian. She says he tried to put his hand up her blouse but she shoved him away because that's off limits on the first snog. I went in behind the mobiles once after the hockey ball. The grass was all trodden down and slimy, littered with cigarette butts and crisp bags, and there was brown water dripping off the roof. It's not really the setting I had in mind for my first kiss.

Geography is my favourite subject. Miss Grange says we're on the same latitude as Canada's Hudson Bay, that it's the Gulf Stream that's stopping us from freezing over like the Arctic. I asked her the name of the white-bellied geese that fly in from Canada in October. I could have googled that but I like asking her things. You can see the Brent geese from the library window, flying in over the Atlantic like an arrow-head. They always look so sure, like they know exactly where they're going. Soon it will be time for them to leave again. I'm always sad to see them go. I don't like the summer, the way everyone strips off into vest tops and shorts and has to be outside all the time. I don't have marks anywhere else on my body, but I still like to stay covered. The outdoors is overrated, if you ask me. I'd much rather be in here, looking out. You can't see things properly when you're moving around, you can't take it all in; you have to be still.

One day Becca brought round her mum's make-up bag and painted concealer all round my mouth. She said I looked great and I should wear it all the time, but when I looked in the mirror I got a real shock, like my whole face had been rubbed out; like those cartoon characters you see on TV when the animator's hand appears with an eraser and wipes them away, limb by limb. I cleaned it off. Becca said I was mad, that nobody would ever go out with me if I didn't make an effort, but I just ignored her. I don't like how the birth mark makes people behave towards me but I don't want to disappear. I can't tell Becca about the text. I think she'd say, 'What would *he* want with *you*?' I think she'd say, 'How do you even know it was him that sent it? How do you know it's not some kind of trap?' I don't. It's alright for her – she'll have other opportunities, she can afford to be sceptical. If I don't go, and he's there, waiting, I'll have blown my chances for good.

Mum used to say that when I was born I was so beautiful that a fairy bent down and kissed me on the mouth and left the imprint there for everyone to see. Even when I was little I knew that wasn't true. It would be a cruel thing for a fairy to do, to leave you a smile that made you sad. I used to beg her to read me 'Briar Rose' every bedtime – the death curse of the old hag at the princess's birth, the thirteenth godmother who lessened it to a sleep, the kiss from the prince that woke her after a hundred years. I used to think that maybe, when I met my prince and he kissed me on the lips, the mark would disappear. But I don't think that anymore. I'm nearly fourteen and I've stopped believing in fairy tales. Like the one where my dad comes back. I don't remember him; he left when I was little, before Mum got sick. Then, after a while, there was just me and Granny. Granny never mentions the mark; it's like she can't see it. She gets really angry if anyone says anything. She's my dad's mum. I think she feels bad about him going. She says Mum and Dad rowed all the time – they couldn't see eye to eye – but I wonder if it was me he couldn't look at. I google him now and again, just to see if he'll turn up somewhere, but so far he hasn't. There aren't many opportunities for a van driver to get in the news.

I don't know what to do about Neil Chambers. I can't ask Granny because I know what she'd say: 'Take nothing to do with a boy who won't be seen with you in public.' If it was a day for

Belle I'd ask her. Belle is our carer. She comes in after I've gone
to school and she gets the shopping and helps Granny do stuff
round the house. She wears rings and bracelets all the way up
her arms and around both her ankles. She jingles wherever she
goes. 'Out she comes as white as snow, rings on her fingers, bells
on her toes.' That's what Granny sings every time she sees her.
Granny thinks it's hilarious because Belle's not white at all, she's
black, but she's very kind and very wise, so she just laughs and
joins in with Granny. Belle gives good advice. When I asked her
about my GCSE choices she said, 'Choose what you love,' so
that's what I did. But she won't be back now till next week and
I won't get a chance to ask her about Neil Chambers. I'm not
stupid. I know he's not a prince. But maybe, if I went, it'd be a
start. You have to make an effort, Becca says.

Our last school trip, to the museum in Belfast, the time Mum
was in hospital, Miss Grange sat beside me the whole way
home. She pointed out the shape of Cavehill to me, how it
looked like a man lying on his back, the peak they call
Napoleon's nose. She said, if there was ever anything I needed
to ask her – about anything, anything at all – I could, and she'd
try to help. But I can't ask her about Neil Chambers. That's not
the kind of thing you can ask a teacher. And anyway, she'd say
behind the mobiles is out of bounds.

Granny's getting slower. Last night, she asked me to wash her
hair. She bent down over the bath and I poured water over her
head from the Tupperware jug. Her scalp was really pink, you
could see the whole shape of her head. When I squeezed the
shampoo out she shouted that it was freezing cold so I lathered
it up quickly and ran my hands behind her ears, over her brow,
as gently as I could. Then I felt a mound at the back of her neck,

and when I looked, there it was – a port wine stain, the same colour and shape as mine, normally hidden by her hair. She must have felt me looking, for she said, 'Don't get water in my ears. Sadie Mulholland got water in her ears one time and it nearly sent her mad. She was never right after it.' So I rinsed off the suds with another jug or two of water and gave her the towel to dry. I didn't know that was who I got it from. She never said.

Granny still comes in to me at night. She squeezes off the switch on my bedside lamp so it doesn't click and wake me, but I hear her, her bones creaking, putting a hand on my shoulder to bid me goodnight. I don't know what will happen to me if anything happens to Granny.

Where is Mr Kenny today? He's usually here by now. If it's the half-Windsor, that's a 'No' as well, less emphatic than a full Windsor, but still a 'No'. The Pratt will be a 'Yes'. Then there's the double cross knot. You have to think twice about that. I'll just wait for a while longer, see if he appears. I don't know what I want it to be.

First Tooth

This is how you lay, little one, the whole night long in my mother's house, with me on my back and you on my chest and your left cheek on mine. I remember I lifted you and laid you in your travel cot, but you were not for travelling. Once the cold of the sheet touched your face, you twisted, opened your eyes, screwed up your fists and cried: cries fit to waken my mother and her mother, and her mother's mother before. I lifted you once, twice, three, four times, lifted you until you taught me what I would not learn: that the only place you wanted to be was next to me, heartbeat to heartbeat, cheek to cheek.

In the morning, my mother looked into my bleary eyes, into eight months of lifting and laying and lifting again. She put her little finger into your small mouth and felt an eruption, the shock of a chip of ivory that had broken the surface: your first tooth. It made sense of everything.

She told me once that after the birth of her ninth child, her doctor had told her to stop birthing children, for the sake of her health. But she didn't stop. She bore another boy, and then me.

'Where would you have been if I'd stopped?' she said to me, and she took your hand, 'And where would this one be?'

I don't know the answer to that. Later, she told me she was annoyed that she had found the tooth, upset at having the glory moment when it was me that had lost sleep over it. Would I not have wished to have found it myself, she said? But who better to have found it, her last baby's first baby's first tooth? Who better but your mother's mother; your own mother, once removed, and not removed at all. We make ourselves over and over again. Your teeth are my teeth, and my bones are hers and her skin is her mother's, and her mother's blood is the blood of hers. Who better to have found your tooth?

'No,' I said, 'I'm not annoyed. You know the rule – the tooth-finder is the cobbler. Now you'll have to buy the first shoes.'

Seven years on and the tooth is jutting straight out of your mouth, dangerously loose, hanging on. It's been like that for weeks. It seems reluctant to go. You won't let me near it, and I'm afraid to touch it. What if it doesn't come free at the first pull? What if something stronger is holding it there? I'm tempted to take you down to see your grandmother – down to the place of the getting of it – and ask her to put her finger once more into your mouth, take a hold again, give the tooth one good tug. I've a good mind to ask her to finish what she started.

Thanks to David Lewis and to Hugh Odling-Smee of Whittrick Press and to the Arts Council of Northern Ireland for its support over the years. Thanks to Averill Buchanan, Debbie McCune, Mandy Taggart and Julie Agnew, and especially to my family Kevin, Mary and Rosie.

Whittrick Press is a (mostly) digital publisher based in
Northern Ireland.

www.whittrickpress.com
twitter.com/whittrickpress